LIFFEY RIVERS

THE ALASKAN SUN

BRENNA BRIGGS

2012

ISBN: 1477510575
ISBN-13: 978-1477510575

There are strange things done in the midnight sun
By the men who moil for gold;
The Arctic trails have their secret tales
That would make your blood turn cold...

--Robert W. Service
"The Cremation Of Sam McGee"

ACKNOWLEDGMENTS
Thanks to Catherine with a 'C' who wanted a polar bear.
Also to Rebecca for her reality checks, Mara and Unateresa
for their technical assistance and Terry for his patient,
helpful editing. Finally, many thanks to Jo Ann Alexander
for her Alaskan cruise ideas and Zack Mac Con Midhe
Warshaw, Donna Barrington and Jim Mueller.

1

The greasy airport nachos Liffey Rivers had wolfed down a few minutes before boarding her flight to Amsterdam were being forcefully ejected from her stomach into the white airsickness bag she held over her face.

While the nachos were punishing her, *Pop Goes the Weasel* kept playing in her head.

Except that in her version, instead of a Jack-in-the-box popping out of its wind-up music box, a huge black mamba snake blasted out and sank its long fangs into her neck.

She tried very hard not to listen to this nursery rhyme tune in her head, but the harder she tried not to listen, the worse it got. So she made up new lyrics:

> **"All around the Johannesburg Feis,**
> **The mamba chased the dancer,**
> **The mamba bared its fangs for flesh,**
> **POP! goes the hamper."**

Detective Powers pretended not to notice that Liffey was throwing up and looked away squeamishly.

Aunt Jean was very concerned and tucked the blanket Mr. Powers had retrieved from the overhead storage locker over Liffey's trembling shoulders.

She reached up to open the air vent and was about to press the flight attendant call button when a muffled "NO!" sounded from the bottom of the paper bag.

Liffey bobbed up and seized her aunt's arm. "I'm fine now, Aunt Jean," she gasped, patting her aunt's hand reassuringly.

She sealed the bag, closed her eyes and began to review the events of the day so far:

'Somewhere on this plane, there is a man who is wearing expensive, hole-punched Italian leather shoes.'

This man had strolled down the aisle immediately after Detective Powers had stood up and reached inside the overhead compartment to get her a blanket and pillow. When Powers had stepped in a bit, to allow the man to get by him, she had recognized the shoes.

Earlier today, at the Johannesburg Feis, she had seen these hole-punched shoes on the man who had delivered a picnic hamper to her outside in a garden, where she was sitting on a bench, hiding out in the hideous safari solo dress her Aunt Jean had designed for her.

A young boy had also been hiding out in the garden.

When she had invited him to eat lunch with her, and had eagerly opened the picnic hamper, which she assumed her father, Robert Rivers, had sent, a huge black mamba snake exploded from it and towered over them.

The snake had attacked the young boy musician in his wheelchair after he bravely positioned himself between the snake and herself to shield her.

After the snake had bitten him twice, it slithered away into the manicured bushes.

Even though young Neil Roberts was now expected to live, he could very well have died on the spot if there had not been a competent doctor at the feis and a trauma center located nearby.

That boy had deliberately sacrificed himself to save her own miserable life.

Now, the same man who had handed her the snake basket at the Johannesburg Feis, was back on the scene.

He was right here on this plane and he had just walked by her in the aisle.

'He must have found out that the black mamba had attacked the wrong person and now he's here to finish the job,' she thought, logically, trying not to completely panic.

'And here I am, sitting next to my Aunt Jean, who is quite possibly the most useless person on earth in any kind of emergency.'

'Finally, we have Steve Powers, the private detective daddy hired to prevent this sort of thing from happening.'

She recalled how earlier today, Detective Powers had let her go off to the Johannesburg Feis by herself so he could watch a rugby match.

'Now, because of me, a little boy in a wheelchair is fighting for his life and I'm next.'

'I think that pretty much sums up the situation,' she thought, resisting a strong impulse to scream.

Liffey bit her lip and opened her tired eyes.

She was overcome with fatigue and the *Pop Goes the Mamba* tune that kept playing over and over in her head.

Today had been the longest day of her life and it was not over yet.

In between listening to the *Weasel* song, she considered what, if any, options she might have up here in this airplane cruising at 58,000 feet.

3

Nothing in particular came to mind, so she leaned back and closed her eyes to avoid looking at the hole-punched shoes when they walked by her again on the way back to their seat.

2

Robert Rivers switched his cell phone over to airplane mode as his law firm's Learjet traveled west. He had responded to his sister Jean's alarming text as best he could and there was nothing more he could do now until his plane touched down in Illinois. He trusted his staff to supervise the safety measures he had orchestrated for his daughter's protection.

He glanced over at his wife, Maeve, and Liffey's friend, Sinead. They were both stretched out and sound asleep across the aisle in the plane's comfortable reclining seats.

Things were going to change now that he was bringing Liffey's mother home after ten long years of believing that she had died in a plane crash. His sister Jean and her 'School of Life' home school teaching methods were going to be terminated. Liffey would not like it, but qualified teachers were going to be hired to tutor her. 'Sending Liffey back to the local schools is no longer possible. It's far too dangerous,' he thought sadly, 'and my sister tries but is inept.'

Mr. Rivers exhaled slowly. The painful reality was that both Liffey and her mother could identify the international smuggler who had already struck at them twice—once on the summit of the mountain in Ireland and then again in South Africa using a professional hit man. His attempts to eliminate Liffey and Maeve had almost succeeded. If his family was ever going to survive, heal and regroup, this man had to be stopped. Permanently. 'No more playing defense and dodging bullets,' Robert Rivers thought. 'From this point on, the Rivers family is playing offense.'

***

Sinead stirred restlessly and willed herself to wake up. It was time to stop thinking about the baby cuckoos and how they were going to push the unsuspecting baby Irish birds out of their nests next spring. She needed to tell Liffey's father that Liffey had been texting her when the snake basket was delivered.

"Mr. Rivers," she hesitated, lowering her voice so as not to wake up Mrs. Rivers, "I think you need to know that Liffey was texting me when that basket with the mamba was delivered to her." Robert Rivers raised his eyebrows.

"Excuse me, Sinead, but are you saying that Liffey was texting you right when that picnic hamper was delivered?"

"Yes, sir."

"Did she say anything about the man who gave it to her?"

"Yes, sir."

Robert Rivers tried not to exhibit signs of his increasing exasperation. Talking to Sinead right now felt like grilling a hostile witness.

"Well then, okay. What did she say about him, Sinead?"

"She said he was wearing brown leather hole-punched shoes like the ones your sister gave you for your birthday last year and you put up for a charity adoption."

"You mean up for auction, Sinead?"

"Yes, Mr. Rivers."

"Did Liffey say anything else, any other little thing that you can remember?"

"No, I'm afraid not."

"All right, then. Thanks very much for this information, Sinead. Try to get some more sleep now. Jet lag can be bad."

***

Robert Rivers immediately stood up and moved to the front of the plane. He picked up the phone on the wall outside the cockpit and dialed Sam Snyder's number.

"Sam, Robert Rivers here again. I need you to get some urgent information to Detective Powers on that flight to Amsterdam you booked."

"Please call him right now. It may already be too late."

"Certainly," Sam said, confident that this was possible because he had already confirmed that Steve Powers had international roaming service.

"If for some reason I cannot get through, I will let you know," Sam said.

"The message is that the man who delivered the snake basket to Liffey today is wearing expensive, brown leather hole-punched shoes."

Sam wondered where Attorney Rivers was going with this. "If this man is on their flight to Amsterdam pursuing Liffey, he may very well be wearing those same shoes."

Sam hoped that his employer was not going to tell him that somebody on Liffey's flight needed to check out all the male passengers' shoes.

"Sam, somebody on that flight needs to check out all of the male passengers' shoes on that plane."

3

'Only 5,400 miles and eleven more hours to go,' Liffey thought grimly, not knowing whether she should laugh or cry.

Even though Liffey was sitting right next to Detective Steve Powers, she felt completely alone. 'It's not likely that the shoe man will make a drastic move for me because it would draw way too much attention to himself and he's probably a professional so he would know better than to do that.'

'If he does come at me, it will be sneaky and quiet. He will make it look like something happened to me due to natural causes.'

Liffey's head was numb. 'Maybe I am freaking out for no good reason. Maybe somebody else is wearing those same shoes? I should have had the nerve to look at him, instead of pretending to be asleep when his shoes walked past me the second time.'

The idea suddenly occurred to Liffey that the delivery man had never seen her without her Irish dance wig.

'I look completely different without my wig. I can check out the passengers on the plane while I'm stretching my legs and see if anyone shows signs of recognizing me, but I'm betting he won't. I can't really 100% identify him either but I think he had a long neck with a big Adam's apple.'

She told Mr. Powers she needed to use the bathroom. She would tell him later, when she returned from her patrol with more information, about her suspicion that the snake delivery man was on this plane for round two. Aunt Jean was sound asleep already, which was good. Sometimes her aunt's chattering drove her crazy.

She moved out into the aisle and faced the front of the cabin, stretching her arms high above her head. After she had carefully studied the occupants of the ten rows of people sitting in the seats in front of her, she determined that the shoe man was not among them and turned around to review the passengers seated behind her.

Liffey was certain that the shoe man was tall and thin. She knew that this plane had a business class section in the front cabin but decided that the shoe man would be too conspicuous if he sat up there. He would have to open the cabin divider and enter the economy cabin to come after her and that would make him stand out.

She began to walk slowly toward the back of the plane where the restrooms were located, casually glancing at each row of passengers as she passed by.

There were three rows of seats across the width of the plane—six seats in the middle and three seats on each side by the windows. It looked to Liffey as if there were about forty rows between the bathrooms at the back and her seat. She was almost certain that the hole-punched shoe man was not sitting in front of her. 'If only I had not wimped out and shut my eyes, I could have watched him returning to his seat.'

After studying each row as best she could, Liffey was astonished that she did not see anyone who even remotely matched her recollection of what the shoe man had looked like. Since she knew he was on this airplane, he had to be hiding from her now.

But how could he have known in advance that she would be walking down the aisle now searching for him? She turned around and carefully scanned the rows in front of her again as she walked back to her seat just in case he had been hiding in the front beverage cart area when she had done her initial front-of-the-cabin check.

Frustrated that she had discovered nothing, she decided to sit down again and think of another plan.

Detective Powers politely stood up and stepped out into the aisle to give her more maneuvering space.

However, before he could sit down again, Mr. Powers was jostled from behind and a man grabbed his shoulders to steady him as he passed by, walking towards the free soft drinks and juice bar service in front of the plane.

"Sorry, 'mahn,'" a baritone voice said apologetically in an accent Liffey did not recognize. He was wearing a light weight, brown leather jacket. Liffey noted the man's long neck and protruding Adam's apple.

She did not get a good look at the man's feet this time and considered that perhaps the pins and needle pricks she was experiencing now might only be due to a bad case of nerves.

But she knew better.

It was him.

For the third time.

She closed her eyes, this time at half-mast, and forced herself to watch the aisle. Shortly, the hole-punched shoes walked slowly by her row to a place behind her that she had not been able to discover during her brief cabin inspection. She could not risk following him or standing up to watch where he went because this man was seriously dangerous. 'He probably has eyes in the back of his head.'

Liffey decided that it was now necessary to confide in Detective Powers. He had honestly admitted to Liffey and her aunt that he was not a very impressive safari guide but assured them he was a competent detective. Liffey was not so sure. Why had he let her go off alone earlier today if he was so competent? Rather than initiate a conversation with Detective Powers in case someone in the seat in front of her might overhear, she took a small notebook out of her backpack and scribbled a short note:

SOS! Mr. Powers, the man who gave me the black mamba basket is on this plane! He is the man who just bumped into you. I recognized him. I am <u>positive</u> it is the same man. We cannot let him know that we know he's here. What do you think we should do????

She tapped Detective Powers on the shoulder. His eyes were closed and he did not respond.

How could he be sleeping already when he had just stood up and allowed her back in to sit down again? 'This is a major emergency so he has *got* to wake up,' she thought irritably, elbowing him hard in his side.

Still no response. Liffey was becoming alarmed.

He was wearing earphones and a sports channel was playing on the screen in front of him. How could he have fallen asleep only seconds after stepping in from the aisle? Especially since she could see that he was apparently watching a soccer game? She could tell that he was still breathing normally because his chest was rising and falling rhythmically. 'Why won't he wake up?'

This was a real life and death situation and her body guard was absent yet again—perhaps not in body this time but certainly in mind and spirit.

'What do I have to do to get his attention?' Liffey pinched him hard on the arm.

Nothing.

Suddenly she felt weak and clammy and electric needles started jabbing at her like she was getting a full body tattoo. She shut her notebook with the SOS message and reached for the airsickness bag.

The terrible reality of what was actually going on here hit her like the time a careless dancer's hard shoe click had connected with the back of her head.

Liffey had noticed that Detective Powers appeared to be thrown a bit off balance when the shoe man came up from behind him. Now it was obvious to her that he had been deliberately bumped from behind when he stepped out into the aisle to let her back in.

'That's what pickpockets do. They try to throw you off balance to distract you. Then they steal your wallet.'

'The shoe man must have injected a sedative, or worse, into Mr. Powers with a small needle when he deliberately slammed into him.'

She had to get this desperate information to her father immediately so he could get through to the air marshal on the plane—if there even was one. Before she located her own phone, Mr. Powers' phone began purring quietly in his shirt pocket.

Some kind of emergency brain alert stopped Liffey from reaching into Detective Powers' pocket to answer his phone or use her own mobile now to call Robert Rivers.

How had the shoe man been able to avoid detection when she had thoroughly searched the entire plane for someone who might resemble him?

Since the plane was only about one fourth full, Liffey was positive that he was not sitting in his seat when she had done her cabin walk-through.

'He *knew* exactly when I stood up and then he must have hidden in one of the restrooms. He's got to be sitting at the very back of this cabin watching me.'

'He must have planted a tiny video camera somewhere close by and he's watching my every move when I am sitting in my seat and if I get up to walk around again, I am going to be the next casualty on this plane.'

The next time the hole-punched shoes walked down the aisle, Liffey knew that she would have to be ready for them, because if she was not ready, there was never going to be a next time.

4

S am dialed Detective Steve Powers and was greatly miffed when Powers did not answer his phone. He had specifically asked this guy if he had international roaming coverage to avoid this kind of phone problem.

He tried Liffey's phone. No answer. As a last resort, he dialed Jean Rivers but the call went to her voice mail.

'Great. Now I get to figure out how I'm supposed to get the hole-punched shoe man message to Powers. Their plane is only a little over an hour out of Johannesburg. I'll call Interpol and ask them to issue an international Red Notice and alert the air marshals on the flight—if there are any, to intercept a man wearing hole-punched shoes for questioning. It's good that Attorney Rivers is working with Interpol's diamond smuggling agents or I would have no idea where to go with this. It sounds completely mental.'

***

'Before I can do anything else, I need to find that camera. If I can disable it, he will not be able to see what I am doing.' Liffey wished now that she was a spy thriller fan because she had absolutely no idea what a miniature surveillance video camera might look like. All she knew was that it had to be very close.

"Use your imagination to construct the unknown, Liffey. It will always delight and surprise you," her father had often told her.

Robert Rivers had also said on many occasions that, "If you yourself can imagine something, you can be almost certain that somebody else has already invented it."

'I need to rerun the scene with Mr. Powers standing in the aisle to let me back in,' Liffey thought. 'His left side would be the logical place for the shoe man to have jabbed him with a small needle. Maybe he planted the camera up on the overhead then too?' Liffey tried her best not to look agitated and totally freaked out.

'Maybe the tiny camera is right here under my nose. Literally. Maybe I don't have to use any imagination at all. I need to examine Mr. Powers' left side without giving it away that I am looking for something.'

A few other disturbing thoughts jumped into Liffey's head: 'What if the shoe man can *hear* me too? What if Aunt Jean wakes up and starts trying to wake Mr. Powers up and then gets all hysterical and draws attention to us? If that happens, the shoe man could rush up here and say he is a doctor and who is going to believe me if I scream for help?'

'I have *got* to find that camera!'

Now that she was certain she was being watched, Liffey performed for the camera. She needed to act carefree.

She reached into her backpack and took out a book about Sangomas that she had purchased in Johannesburg.

She tried to read it but could not get her eyes to focus.

She yawned and stretched, moving her squinty, pretend-sleepy-eyes over the compartment area above Detective Powers.

Liffey tried not to obviously react when she spotted a small beige button-like object attached next to the air vent control button. It was so tiny she could hardly believe she had seen it.

'So it's official then. I am being watched by a *button*? And if I don't disable the button, my chances of arriving safely in Amsterdam are about zero, not to mention the fact that I also need to get Detective Powers some medical help.'

'If I call the cabin crew and show them the button and tell them about the shoe man, they will think I am playing some kind of childish spy game. I have to disable the button camera myself, right now, and then call daddy.'

Liffey yawned and rubbed her eyes. She did head rolls left to right and right to left six times. Then she stood up, struggling to climb over detective Powers' long, immobile legs.

She reached above her head and positioned her hands on the overhead compartment, acting like she was trying to steady herself, while she scraped her left palm like a butter knife over the little button.

It fell silently to the floor in between Detective Powers' feet. She felt for it under her left foot sneaker and squashed it like a bug.

To make sure that the shoe man did not think she had deliberately interrupted his surveillance, Liffey stepped out into the aisle nonchalantly and slowly opened the overhead locker and removed her hard shoes from her dance bag.

Realizing she probably only had a matter of minutes, if that, before the shoe man would figure out what she had done, deliberately or not, she shut the storage unit and scrambled back over Mr. Powers to her seat.

She removed her cross-trainer sneakers and had the leather straps buckled on her hard shoes in less than thirty seconds.

Her bare feet felt sticky and sweaty in the tight leather shoes but she would not be needing them to walk.

She would be needing the heels of the hard shoes to kick the kneecaps of the hole-punched shoe man when he came at her again.

After her hard shoes felt secure, she dialed her father, hoping the assassin had not placed another mini camera-microphone in her vicinity.

'Poor daddy,' she thought sadly. 'He hasn't had much good news lately.'

5

Maeve McDermott Rivers shivered. She felt cold and that *never* happened. Where were the beautiful coal-black women dressed in white and why was she sitting in this small airplane?

This was not the medical transport plane. She looked around anxiously and watched the handsome man talking on the phone directly in front of her.

He was shouting orders into it like a general in a war zone. She would be still and listen until she could figure out what was going on.

"First, you must keep your head down, Liffey. It's good you have your hard shoes on for kicking, but if he's quick, and he will be, they might not be enough. You need to have something prepared to throw in his face to distract him before you have a go at him."

There was a pause after which Robert Rivers laughed nervously.

"A full airsickness bag sounds perfect. The contents are harmless but disgusting and he will instinctively recoil with revulsion when he realizes what you have thrown at his face. This will buy you some valuable seconds and allow you to position yourself advantageously in the aisle. You need to hit him right in the eyes with the vomit, Liffey, and then immediately kick him hard on both of his knee caps."

"After you kick him, you should have some outside help. Sam Snyder is on it and I have personally called the airline to alert them about your precarious predicament."

'That man knows that something is wrong too,' Maeve strained to eavesdrop over the engine.

She saw that there was a young girl sleeping peacefully across the aisle from her but it was not Liffey. She tried to remember how she had gotten on this airplane and where she was going but everything was all muddled up as usual.

It was exhausting always trying to remember things. Her head felt like it weighed a hundred pounds.

Nothing made any sense but she remembered she knew this man on the phone and that she trusted him. If she could just shake off this feeling of dread, she would talk to him after he was done with his phone call. He appeared to be very upset.

***

Sam Snyder knew it had only been ten minutes since he had contacted Interpol but it seemed like it had been hours. What was taking them so long to find out if there were air marshals on Liffey's flight?

'When I talk to that Powers idiot again, I am not going to be polite.'

After fifteen minutes, it dawned on him that he should probably stop holding his breath waiting for a follow-up phone call from Interpol. 'Maybe they won't be getting back to me about whether or not there are marshals on the plane. That information is probably classified.'

***

Liffey gave her Aunt Jean a nervous little squeeze on the arm and tried to summon up enough courage for the task ahead. She shut her eyes so the tears she could feel welling up behind her eyelids would not come flooding down her face. 'It is so good she is still sleeping,' Liffey thought, drawing in a deep breath. 'There is no way Aunt Jean would ever get over it if she saw me throwing throw-up from this disgusting airsickness bag at someone's face!'

Detective Powers still seemed to be sleeping, but Liffey was very concerned. His breathing had become shallower and a bit uneven.

'I need to step up this shoe man meeting,' she thought, climbing over Detective Powers and jumping into the aisle. She said a quick prayer and reminded herself not to become completely unglued.

'This should get him interested.' Liffey bit her lip and fell forward into a rag doll stretch, her body facing the front of the cabin and her head dangling down between her legs, looking behind her.

She was acutely aware that while she was waiting for this inevitable, terrifying confrontation, she was experiencing a rush of adrenaline.

Her muscles felt like taut violin strings that would make a high pitched ping when she moved.

With her head almost touching the floor, she tried to focus clearly on the aisle in back of her. 'Who would have ever guessed that these stretches would be so useful?'

The open airsickness bag was carefully placed on Mr. Powers' lap where she could quickly get at it.

Liffey did not have to hang upside down for long. Within seconds, she saw the hole-punched shoes walking down the aisle toward her at a leisurely pace. She knew she would have to time things perfectly if this surreal plot was going to work.

When she thought the shoes were slowing down, she began to unfold herself and get into position. Liffey knew that if she let this man tap her from behind, indicating he wanted to pass by her, this 'tap' would include an injection of something she did not even want to think about.

The shoe man had wanted Detective Powers to go to sleep. He wanted Liffey Rivers to be dead and probably did not even know why. He was being paid to get rid of her by a man who, according to her father, was the most ruthless conflict diamond smuggler in Africa. "You can identify him, Liffey, and so can your mother. That's why he keeps coming after both of you."

When Liffey was certain that the shoe man was in target range, she spun around, snatched the open airsickness bag from Detective Powers' lap and hurled the undigested, sludgy nachos at the shoe man's face like she was putting out a campfire with a bucket of water.

He cried out, "What the...?" Then he stepped back, outraged, automatically reaching for his face to wipe off the nacho slime just as she had hoped he would, allowing her time to deliver two powerful snap kicks to both knee caps, which brought him down hard to the floor on his right side.

A loud chorus of disgust rose up from the passengers in the vicinity and in the midst of it, she heard a loud scream coming from Aunt Jean: "Liffey what are you DOING? What has come over you?"

The man lying on the floor called Liffey, "psycho" and "crazy," as passengers on both sides of the aisle rallied around him to help him get back up on his feet.

"Aunt Jean!" Liffey shouted over the din, "look at Detective Powers! He is out cold now because this man injected him with something. He is the same man who tried to kill me today at the feis with the black mamba."

"Just try to wake up Mr. Powers! He *can't* wake up because this man injected him with a sedative right after the plane took off so he would not be able to protect us."

Aunt Jean tried unsuccessfully to wake up Detective Powers.

The event in the aisle caused some heated discussion among the passengers who were still trying to get the man lying in the aisle back up on to his feet.

"This crazy girl probably knocked both men out," is what Liffey was dismayed to be hearing from the crowd more than anything else. It was obvious that most of them thought that after she had drugged the man in the seat next to her, she had immediately attacked the nice looking young man now lying on the floor who was only trying to politely move past her.

It was also apparent to Liffey that something drastic had happened to the shoe man which was way beyond the pain she had caused to his kneecaps. He had gone completely limp and appeared to be unconscious.

"What have you *done* to this poor, innocent man?" a hostile looking older woman with bright red hair that matched her lipstick demanded as she continued her efforts to pull the hole-punched shoe man up. "Somebody *please* get some medical help here!" she demanded.

"Check his hands," Liffey said calmly. "You will find a small syringe needle in one of them that was meant for me. But whatever you do, do NOT let the needle jab you or you will die!"

"You obviously watch way too much stupid television," interjected a furious man in an expensive tan sport jacket who was leaning over his seat watching the drama unfold.

"Please, just check his hands," Liffey said again. She could not believe how composed she sounded because she felt sick to her stomach and was fairly certain she was going to need a new airsickness bag any second now.

"There is no needle in either one of his hands," the red-lipped woman reported after a quick assessment.

"Where is the cabin crew?" someone shouted from the crowd.

"Probably getting tea sorted out," a thick male British accent answered.

"Somebody needs to get this girl under control before she strikes again," the red-lipped, hostile woman advised, pointing directly at Liffey.

Liffey grimaced when she saw that most of the people who were not standing up gawking at her now, were sitting down texting about what had just happened.

"This is so bad," Liffey said to herself. "Where are the air marshals? They were supposed to handle this."

A dignified looking, salt-and-pepper haired man, moved through the pack of people surrounding the hole-punched shoes man. He said he was a doctor and winced slightly when he noted the nacho slime covering the face of the man lying on the floor.

"What is it that has happened here? What's all this about a needle?" he asked.

Liffey tried to explain, "Doctor, I don't know why the needle he was going to inject me with is not in one of his hands."

Pointing over to Detective Powers, who was obviously unconscious, slumped far down in his seat, she said, "The man lying here on the floor, disabled that man over there sleeping in his seat who is a detective traveling with me and my aunt. I am absolutely certain that the man on the floor was about to inject me with something lethal because he tried to kill me earlier today in Johannesburg when he delivered a black mamba snake to me in a picnic basket at an Irish dancing competition."

"Oh for pity's sake!" a disembodied male voice roared. "Don't believe a word this girl says. She is *certified*. First, she throws vomit on this poor man and then she kicks him unconscious!"

"I did *not* kick his head!" Liffey protested. "I only kicked his kneecaps to stop him from stabbing me with a needle."

"You have got to be kidding, right?" a young woman piped up. "What is *wrong* with you anyway? Get a life!"

"Well, I guess we don't have any air marshals on this flight or they would have certainly stepped in and stopped this vicious, unprovoked attack," another bodiless voice shouted.

"Everybody just hold your horses now," the doctor said as he painstakingly removed the vomit from the downed man's face. "I can see a small syringe needle protruding from his neck. It must have punctured the carotid artery when he instinctively tried to wipe the emesis off his face, which, I have gathered from what you have all told me, the young lady here tossed at him."

"What kind of raging lunatic would throw a barf bag at a stranger on a plane?" a voice called out from the very back of the plane.

"How do we know that this crazy girl did not stab him in the neck?" the persistent red-lipped woman demanded.

"How could she be throwing vomit in his face while she was also stabbing him in the neck and kicking him?" a lone, sympathetic voice asked from somewhere in the middle of the group of people who had now moved in at close range.

"Doctor, be careful with that needle, it's lethal!" Liffey cried out. "And please take a look at this man here in the aisle seat next to me. He needs medical attention."

The doctor looked over and saw that Detective Powers appeared to be unconscious. He stood up and opened one of Powers' eyes with his thumb. Then he did the same thing to the man lying on the floor before he made a startling announcement:

"The man on the floor is in shock and experiencing circulatory collapse. We must summon the cabin crew immediately and the captain of this plane will have to enforce protocol."

The doctor took a handkerchief from his pocket and carefully wrapped it around the needle and asked if anyone had an envelope to preserve the evidence. He examined the shoe man's coat pockets and removed a vial of clear liquid.

"This is labeled *Dendroaspis Polylepis* which indicates it is from the black mamba snake. But I cannot tell whether it is the antivenom for emergency snake bite treatment or the actual poisonous venom milked from the snake."

"It's the venom," Liffey said quietly. "I'm sure of it."

"I am afraid that we will need to return to Johannesburg immediately as there are two men on this plane now who need emergency medical attention," the doctor proclaimed.

This proclamation by the doctor made the passengers complain loudly but he carried on resignedly. "Are there any other medical personnel on this flight? I could use some help here."

Liffey was weak from fear and completely drained from her ordeal but the people around her did not seem even remotely interested in her well-being. 'They actually seem to seriously think that I had something to do with this man's collapse!' she thought incredulously.

Finally, two cabin stewards made their way through the noisy, irate crowd and asked if there was a "Liffey Rivers" in the group. Liffey reluctantly raised her hand. When they saw the man lying on the floor, one of them said, "I hope

25

you are all right, Miss Rivers? We were in the galley heating up supper when the captain told us to find you immediately and bring you up to the cockpit for the duration of our flight. I guess we were a little late but it looks like you handled things brilliantly."

"I was just lucky," Liffey said, managing an anemic smile. Aunt Jean eventually pushed her way through the people blocking her. "This is all completely unacceptable, Liffey! How much more can we be expected to endure in one day? And just look at Mr. Powers. Doctor! Please direct your attention to this good man over here at once and leave that would be assassin on the floor for the time being."

Liffey was impressed that her aunt seemed to be taking charge for a change and was acting on behalf of Detective Powers. The doctor complied. He stood up slowly, moved passed Liffey over to the unconscious man in the seat and took his pulse. Then he opened the detective's eyes and looked at both pupils.

"He's been drugged all right, young lady."

Aunt Jean automatically assumed that the doctor was addressing her and blushed."Well, people do tell me that I look younger than I am, Doctor," she said appreciatively. Liffey smothered a groan. In the middle of all this chaos, Aunt Jean was, as usual, thinking about how she looked.

After the doctor had placed several blankets over the unconscious man on the floor, he said that he needed to speak with the captain and walked towards the cockpit.

'I wonder how much the shoe man was paid to get rid of me?' Liffey contemplated. 'All I wanted to do today was to dance at the feis in Johannesburg. Now, little Neil is on life support, Mr. Powers has been drugged and everybody on this plane thinks I am a dangerous head case because I injured a man who was trying to murder me.'

Shortly after the doctor left for a consultation with the captain, an unwelcome, but expected announcement, came from the cockpit: "Ladies and gentlemen, may I have your attention, please. This is your captain speaking. Due to unforeseen medical emergencies, I regret to inform you that we are returning to Johannesburg."

The uproar on the plane was instantaneous. Furious passengers hurled insults at Liffey as the stewards ushered her quickly up to the cockpit. 'Like all of this is *my* fault?' Liffey fumed.

Aunt Jean stayed with Detective Powers.

The doctor returned from the front of the plane with a manual respirator from the emergency equipment closet and attached it to the shoe man's chest. A young missionary nun in a light brown habit had stationed herself by the man on the floor. She offered to operate the breathing apparatus for the doctor while he examined the man further.

After observing the barely alive man's excessive sweating and the saliva drooling from his mouth, she whispered, "I think this man is symptomatic for snake bite, Doctor."

"So do I, Sister. So do I."

6

The man sitting in the small, nondescript corner café in Johannesburg, doused his smelly cigar in a half-empty cup of tepid coffee and stood up excitedly. An animated woman broadcaster onsite at Oliver Tambo Airport had an exclusive report from a passenger on Flight 802 to Amsterdam that the plane was now heading back to Johannesburg with two critically ill passengers.

"Unconfirmed texts from passengers on Flight 802 have indicated that foul play is strongly suspected and that a young girl is involved."

The man lit another cigar, signaled for his waiter, and asked in halting English that a bottle of champagne be brought to his table. Plan B had obviously worked. His agent had informed him that the black mamba had bitten the wrong person at the feis but that he was prepared to finish the job on a flight to Amsterdam that Liffey Rivers had booked.

'At last,' he gloated. 'Time to celebrate. That plane will not make it back in time for anyone to figure out what happened to the wig girl. How sad.'

'One down, one to go,' he thought happily. 'As soon as her mother is gone, there will be no one left on earth who can connect all the dots.'

He smiled congenially at his waiter who was pouring cheap white bubbly into a royal blue plastic champagne flute.

***

Sam Snyder slumped down on his sagging couch after his conversation with Robert Rivers had ended on a sour note.

Attorney Rivers had reminded him that, "All or at least most of this fiasco could have been prevented."

Sam cringed and recapped the events in his head. First off, he should have told his boss that he had decided not to go to New York. 'But how was I supposed to know Liffey and her dizzy aunt were planning to run off to South Africa? At least I managed to trace them to the elephant reserve where they stayed. And I did hire Detective Powers to cover them in South Africa. How could I have guessed he would ditch Liffey's Irish dance competition to watch a rugby game instead back at his hotel? And then, after a black mamba almost kills Liffey because Powers is not there to inspect the picnic basket delivered to her, he manages to get tagged on the plane to Amsterdam after take-off. No wonder Attorney Rivers is furious. At least my boss is the one who told me to hire Powers again to accompany them on the trip back to Chicago. It is hard to believe Liffey managed to take out that guy by herself. Who would believe a kid could do that?'

***

"Miss Rivers, I am Captain Jack Sparrow," said a thick South African voice belonging to a strikingly handsome man with light green eyes and eyebrows as bushy as the hedges in Liffey's front yard.

Liffey smiled and extended her hand for a 'How do you do?' handshake.

Either Captain Jack Sparrow did not know what an introductory handshake was, or he pretended not to notice because he did not offer his own hand. 'Maybe he has some kind of fear of germs and won't touch anything,' Liffey thought, her eyes scanning the inside of the cockpit which reminded her of an interactive video game in a shopping mall arcade.

There were panels of tiny lights above her and dials and knobs and levers and joy sticks and little computer screens. She felt like Alice who had just fallen down the rabbit hole into Computer Wonderland where, instead of the White Rabbit and Mad Hatter, there was Captain Jack Sparrow.

The way this day had been going so far, it seemed perfectly logical that there was a Captain Jack Sparrow in charge of this flight.

Even though the captain looked nothing like a pirate from the Caribbean, Liffey considered making a smart-aleck observation and saying something like, "Why did you cut off your dreadlocks, Captain?" but decided not to risk irritating him and being sent back to her seat, which would mean she would have to pass by several rows of menacing passengers.

"I have been briefed about your situation with regard to the two men on board who are in critical condition. We are returning to Oliver Tambo Airport as I speak."

Liffey could tell that the plane was adjusting its altitude and was beginning to descend and bank left.

"I regret that my crew was not there to aid you when the man with the needle presented himself."

Liffey thought too that it would have been very nice if someone had 'presented' themselves to help her subdue the shoe man.

"I got the call from Tambo Control Tower that you were in immediate danger shortly after you had already handled the situation by yourself, and I do apologize for that, Miss Rivers."

"Well, no hard feelings, Captain Sparrow," Liffey replied cheerfully.

"Good," Captain Sparrow said indifferently.

"Whew," Liffey rolled her eyes. Black mambas, Captain Jack Sparrow... She was back home again in her familiar home away from home. The Twilight Zone.

7

Louise Anderson stared apprehensively out her hotel window, sipping her morning coffee and wondering if she had made the right decision to cancel her return flight to St. Louis tonight. After bringing her up to speed about the events at the feis in Johannesburg and the incident on the airplane, Robert Rivers had persuaded her to intercept Liffey and Jean at the airport in Amsterdam and accompany them back to the States.

Before Robert Rivers' phone call a few minutes ago, she had planned to do the Red Brick walking tour of Boston's historical district before her conference later this afternoon. After the meeting, she had a dinner reservation at Papa's, the Italian restaurant with the huge meatballs Liffey was always talking about.

If Attorney Rivers had not sounded so desperate when they talked, she probably would have declined. Now there was barely enough time to make it to the airport, but he had already booked the flight and a limo to pick her up.

It had been months since she had lost Liffey's trail in Wisconsin after she had set off a fire alarm at her middle school and taken a shuttle bus to O'Hare Airport where she had somehow managed to board a flight to Dublin. It was good to know that Attorney Rivers apparently did not blame her for Liffey's escape.

Someday, she would tell Robert Rivers how close his daughter had come to catastrophe in St. Louis, the first time he had hired her to protect his daughter. 'If I had not followed Liffey into that hotel stairwell and tripped the man who was racing down the steps after her, there might have been a very different outcome,' she thought.

Sometimes she could still hear Liffey screaming from several floors below after the man had painfully scrambled up from the stairwell's cement floor and abandoned his pursuit.

'If only Liffey were not able to identify him...'

'I'm going to request trans-Atlantic air marshal support on the Amsterdam-Chicago flight,' she decided.

'When the media in Johannesburg reports that Liffey is still alive and healthy, it's pretty obvious what that man will try to do next.'

"Next!" she cried out, "*of course!*"

"What took me so long to see what is *next?*"

'There is no way Liffey can get on another plane now. She must be placed in emergency custody immediately. There's got to be a leak!'

'How could it be a coincidence that the same man who had delivered the black mamba to Liffey earlier today was apparently now on the same plane Liffey was taking to Amsterdam?'

'Somebody obviously had *told* him. That's how.'

'Liffey needs to be placed in protective custody while she's still at the airport.'

8

Even though Liffey was enjoying sitting in the jump seat behind the first officer as the plane pushed away thick white cloud banks like a giant snow plow, she fell asleep.

She woke up when the landing gear thudded down into position and the wing flaps began to slow the plane down.

"Fasten your seatbelt, Liffey," Captain Sparrow called out over the whining computers programmed to land the plane."We are in touch with Approach Control now and will be landing at OT in approximately ten minutes."

Liffey usually dreaded the shrill landing noise made by a large plane beginning its descent, but watching Captain Sparrow and his co-pilot manipulating all the instrument panels distracted her, and soon she felt the plane touching smoothly down on the runway.

"May I please return to my seat now, Captain Sparrow?"

"Sorry, Miss Rivers. You will need to remain here until the paramedics remove the two critically ill passengers and the local Gauteng police detectives take your statement. They will also be interviewing eyewitness passengers while their forensic team gathers evidence."

"Before you make a statement, you may wish to contact your family's attorney if you have one."

Liffey wanted to scream! 'I'm the one who's almost murdered on this plane and *I'm* treated like the criminal? Does Captain Sparrow think I'm some kind of homicidal maniac?'

The plane slowly taxied up to the terminal and Captain Sparrow announced: "Your attention, please. This is your captain speaking. I regret to inform you that we will be delayed while our critically ill passengers are removed from the plane by paramedics after which the police will be conducting a formal investigation into the circumstances surrounding these unexpected events. Please be cooperative with the local authorities so that we may resume our flight to Amsterdam as soon as possible."

Before Liffey could think of a convincing argument to let her out of the cockpit to reunite with her aunt, the door opened and two men in sun glasses and dark suits entered.

"If you don't mind, Captain, we would like to speak to this young lady privately?" one of them said.

Captain Sparrow was noticeably annoyed when the men flashed their Interpol badges and ushered Co-Pilot Miley and himself out of the cockpit.

Liffey took a deep breath and tried to prepare herself mentally for the grilling to come from the two suits. But to her surprise, instead of firing questions at her, the two men in suits abruptly left and Aunt Jean walked in surrounded by four uniformed local police officers.

"Liffey, darling, here is your backpack. You'll be happy to know that Detective Powers is showing signs of waking up, and your shoe man remains in his coma."

"All right then ladies. It's time to go," said an impatient young woman police officer.

"You mean I don't have to answer a million questions first?" Liffey asked, grateful that she was apparently being let off the hook again.

"I don't know anything about that," the officer replied crisply. "My orders are to get you off this plane immediately and turn you over to airport security."

"What happens then?" Liffey asked.

"I guess you'll just have to wait until you find out," was the snippy reply.

"Okay, then I guess we should just go and turn me over to airport security."

"Good idea," answered the police woman as she placed a small white see-through veil over Liffey's face.

"Both of you will need to link arms and walk quickly side by side as we proceed into the terminal. Look straight ahead and do not speak to one another." Aunt Jean was about to object when the police officers formed a human shield and began to move them out through the plane's exit door and down a long ramp.

At the end of the ramp leading directly into the arrival gate lounge, she could see flashing lights and what looked like an army of blue uniformed police wearing riot helmets and vests that said: POLICE.

Aunt Jean threw her shoulders back and perked up. "Let's get ready for our public, darling! I would have liked to have seen these officers just try to cover up *my* face!"

Aunt Jean! You don't get it," Liffey muttered under her breath."We don't *want* all this attention. Try to remember what is going on here! That man on the plane drugged Detective Powers and then he tried to kill me. And if the man that hired him to do it finds out that I am not dead, he will come after me again. This is terrible!"

"Well, Liffey, dear, when life gives us lemons, we must always make lemonade."

"So true, Aunt Jean, but when life gives you snakes in picnic hampers and hit men on airplanes, you need to try to become invisible." Aunt Jean smiled tolerantly, brushed her hair back and waved to the cameras lined up behind the police barricades.

"So, who *are* we dealing with here?" one of the police officers asked after they had passed by the media circus.

"Not sure but Interpol is very, very interested, so I am thinking we have something big going on," another voice remarked.

"How big?" two voices shouted.

"Like the 'Raven' big," another voice answered.

This new information seemed to take the wind out of the police shield's wings and they slowed down.

"The Raven? That's just great. I was hoping to live until after the semi-finals match tonight," a deflated voice said.

"Shush! Please keep it down!" the voice belonging to the irritable woman who had placed the veil over Liffey's face ordered.

'They don't want us to understand what they are talking about,' Liffey thought anxiously as the police conversation abruptly switched from English to Afrikaans.

Liffey wished she could disappear when she recognized a familiar Afrikaans word one of the police officers used as they plodded along towards the Airport Security Office.

"De Slang."

"You're kidding, right?" an officer who had apparently forgotten that they had switched to Afrikaans said in a loud English whisper.

"The Snake is the man this girl took out? Unbelievable! He's been at the top of our 'Most Wanted' list for years."

9

The man sitting at the chrome-trimmed, blue Formica table in the nondescript corner café, stubbed his second smelly cigar out in an empty glass.

He was accustomed to the finer things in life and it was unthinkable to celebrate his success today with this disgusting, so-called champagne he had ordered. It tasted more like cleaning fluid.

"Garçon, l'addition s'il vous plait," he said impatiently.

Today he was French. He had learned many languages over the years and was fairly comfortable speaking French, even though English was his native tongue.

Since his business dealings and very survival depended on anonymity, he had recently subjected himself to a third nose reconstruction surgery while he continued to recover from his unfortunate mishap in Ireland.

At times it was quite difficult trying to keep all of his lies straight. He used many aliases to move diamonds out of Africa, 'relocate' great works of art from museums and supervise production at his oil fields throughout the world.

This latest transformation into a French tourist gave him an everyman kind of look which he liked. He now had a good, solid nose. Not too long and not too short. Nothing like the pointed, beaky nose he had been born with. His mother had nicknamed him 'Raven' when his shiny black hair came in and replaced the baby fuzz on his head.

He congratulated himself for having hired the most reliable hit man in the western hemisphere. Apparently, it had paid off.

He smiled broadly as the waiter handed him his check. "In this life, you always get what you pay for, son," he said in a thick French accent.

"Your cheap house champagne is terrible! Champagne *pas cher*! It tastes like battery acid, and…" He was about to continue this "you get what you pay for" lecture when the football match on television was interrupted again with a live update on the passenger incidents which had occurred on the Johannesburg flight to Amsterdam.

"Two critically ill male passengers are being transferred now by paramedics to waiting ambulances at Oliver Tambo International Airport," a somber-voiced man reported.

The camera panned over to emergency stretchers being wheeled quickly away from the passenger gate area over to waiting ambulances.

When the words 'male' and 'passengers' registered in his head, he sat down stiffly, trying to control the involuntary twitching he could feel starting up on the right side of his face.

"If you want something done right, son, then you must always do it yourself," he said, matter-of-factly, trying to keep his composure.

The waiter became alarmed and backed up a step when he saw his customer's face begin to contort with rage and heard throaty, "*kraw, kraw*," crow-like noises erupting from his throat like uncontrollable hiccups.

The waiter watched nervously as the French tourist pulled a sizable wad of Rand from his wallet and slammed the money down on the table.

"Keep the change," the customer croaked.

Thoughts were galloping through the French tourist's head. The only problem with this do-it-yourself line of reasoning was that he had already *tried* to do it himself, more than once, with terrible results. All he had managed to accomplish trying to take care of things himself in Ireland was to almost die and probably permanently injure his right arm.

The fact that he had not died when the strong black horse had bucked and thrown him over the cliff was due only to the fact that he had landed on the top of a cluster of soft needled pine trees. The branches had stopped his fall into the abyss below.

Outside of the café, he removed his mobile phone from his yellow polo shirt pocket with his left hand and dialed a number that he had memorized but not used in several years.

After listening to instructions from the taped recording on the other end of the phone, he pressed the #9 option. "Superintendent Johnson," an efficient, no-nonsense voice answered.

"This is Monsieur Poinsette," he said in a thick French accent, "I am in need of police assistance immediately at Oliver Tambo Airport."

"Just one moment, please, Monsieur Poinsette, let me transfer you to the front desk."

Superintendent Johnson disconnected his office call and quickly took out his private mobile phone. 'Well,' he thought, 'This is interesting. It's been a long time since the Raven has asked for my assistance.'

***

When Liffey and her aunt finally reached the Oliver Tambo Airport Security Office, they were concerned when the tight police shield which had accompanied them from the plane and all the way through the terminal, suddenly scattered like a kaleidoscope image, leaving them alone and unprotected in the empty security office.

Aunt Jean broke the silence. "This is certainly surprising, Liffey. After being totally smothered by security forces, we are now sitting all alone in the ugliest office I have ever seen."

Pins and needles began to creep up and down Liffey's arms. Aunt Jean was right. Why *was* it that, after all the 'protection,' they were now completely alone? A phone vibration in her jacket pocket interrupted Liffey's tingling premonition of an impending doom. She had turned it off on the plane when she realized that something bad had happened to Detective Powers and she was probably being watched.

"Liffey, this is Louise. No time to explain. Where are you?"

"Johannesburg, in the Oliver Tambo Airport Security Office."

"Is anyone with you?"

"Just Aunt Jean."

"Good. Okay then, Liffey. Listen up! This is what you need to do."

Liffey could not believe she was being told now by an obviously very tense Louise that she had to "do" something else. 'How many things is a 13-year-old girl expected to *do all by herself* just to survive in one twenty-four hour period?'

She tried hard not to accept an invitation to a self-pity party.

"Liffey, you can't trust anyone now. Do you understand what I'm saying? You cannot trust *anyone*, no matter who they are or say they are or seem to be. Do you understand?"

"I guess so, but what does that mean? What am I supposed to do here in South Africa not trusting *anyone*?"

"I cannot believe I'm saying this but you have to set off another fire alarm and get out of the airport. Head for the main terminal entrance as soon as it goes off."

"Are you serious?"

"I'm afraid so, and we both know that you know how to activate fire alarms."

"Your security at the airport on at least one, and possibly even several levels, has now been compromised. After his botched hit at the feis, the man on the plane who assaulted you had to have been told by someone that you would be on that Amsterdam flight. You need to immediately get out of that office with your aunt and blend in with the crowd. Do you happen to have one of your wigs with you?"

"Actually, I do. The blonde one I wore in New York, when I was posing as Siobhan McKenna at the Liberty Torch Feis, is still in my backpack." Louise had no idea who Siobhan McKenna was and why Liffey had been posing as her, but said, "Good. Put that wig on right now and then get that fire alarm going."

"Outside the airport, the U.S. Consulate General in Johannesburg has arranged for a green limo to take you back to their headquarters where they will arrange safe passage out of the country for you and your aunt. Any other way is far too risky. Is there a fire alarm nearby?"

"Yes. Actually, I see one right inside the door in front of me."

"Good. Now go and do whatever you need to do and then you and your aunt get out. Stay as close to the middle of the crowd as you can and work your way out of the terminal through the main entrance where the limo will be waiting for you. Do not look around or behind you before you leave the terminal. The driver has been instructed to get you out of there like a race car driver at the finish line. U.S. Consulate security will meet you off the road at the second airport exit and you will switch cars and go back to Johannesburg with them."

"Okay. I'm on it, Louise. Thanks."

"Call me when you make contact with the Consulate General."

"I will."

"Then call your father. He's a mess."

"I will."

Pulling the matted blonde wig out from the bottom of her backpack, Liffey turned to her aunt and said, "Aunt Jean, could you please help me put this wig you gave me on properly? It's hard without a mirror."

"Certainly, Liffey, darling. Although after that horrible old woman ripped it off your head in New York, I am surprised you want to wear it again."

"You know, Liffey, after we get out of this dreadful place, we can make you permanently blonde if you like. My colorist would be delighted. In fact, maybe I will give her a call right now and…"

10

Sinead McGowan had been trying to sleep on the plane because she did not want anyone to feel like they had to entertain her.

She could tell that there seemed to be a big problem of some kind but could not make out what is was from across the aisle.

Without drawing attention to herself, she found her mobile phone. 'Am I dreaming, or did I hear Mrs. Rivers talking to Mr. Rivers like she is a regular, normal person?'

At Sligo General Hospital, Sinead had never had what could be considered anything close to resembling a normal conversation with Mrs. Rivers.

***

Liffey was inspecting herself in Aunt Jean's compact mirror, after positioning her blonde wig on her head as best she could with only a few bobby pins. She was glad that there was a fire alarm box located just a few feet away near the door.

She took a deep breath, instructed Aunt Jean to gather up all their things and placed her hand on the door knob,

44

hoping there would not be a guard posted outside in the hallway.

Her phone began vibrating again.

It was Sinead.

'Now what?' she thought.

"Sinead?"

"Liffey, I've been desperately wanting to talk to you about Africa…"

"I really can't talk, now Sinead. I'll call you back as soon as I can. Promise."

Before Sinead could get another word out, Liffey hung up.

Sinead was used to Liffey's somewhat rude abruptness by now and did not take offense. There seemed to be so much going on at the moment. It was making her head spin.

'Maybe I should not risk talking to Liffey now anyway,' she thought. 'I might slip up and tell her I am with her parents and ruin the surprise.'

She reached into her bag and took out two more pills to ease the stabbing pain in her head. Maybe when they got to the States, she would ask Mr. Rivers to take her to a doctor to get a prescription for more powerful pain medication.

She was not sure how much longer she could endure this constant headache.

***

The Intensive Care Unit in the Johannesburg hospital was buzzing when Neil Roberts returned to consciousness.

Could he feel his toes moving?

'I'm dreaming,' he thought. 'I can't move my toes. I wouldn't even know how it *feels* to move my toes.'

Curiosity surfaced in his groggy head and he decided not to remain in this pleasant dream-like state.

He wanted to have a look at his feet. He used his elbows to prop himself up and managed to move his legs over the edge of the bed which immediately set off noisy alarms and flashing lights.

A group of three ICU nurses came rushing into his room.

They stopped in their tracks when they observed their young, paralyzed patient kicking his thin, muscle-atrophied legs back and forth over the side of the bed, wiggling his toes.

***

The Intensive Care Unit staff had seen remarkable things over their collective seventy-five years of working there, but nothing like what was happening before their eyes right now.

This young boy had miraculously survived two deep fang bites from a black mamba snake which normally would have injected enough venom into him to have killed twenty-nine full grown men.

Somehow, Neil Roberts was now not only not dead, he was moving his paralyzed limbs and wiggling his toes

Senior Nurse Greene instructed her assistants to remain calm even though she herself had dropped her clipboard when she had seen him moving.

She abruptly left the room and dialed the ICU physician on call, the staff pediatric neurologist and four of the resident physicians on duty.

She also called Sister Helen, who had finally left her ward's side to check back in at her orphanage and possibly get a few hours sleep.

She left voice mail:

"Sister Helen, this is Rose Greene in ICU. I am calling to inform you that Neil is sitting up in bed fully conscious. He is also moving his legs and toes."

Next, she contacted the on-call snake bite consultant who happened to be on the hospital premises with another seriously ill snake bite victim.

Finally, she dialed Liffey Rivers, the Irish dancer from America Neil had protected from the black mamba. Liffey had made her promise to call when there was any change in her young hero's condition, either way—good or bad.

'Miracles really do happen,' she thought.

'There is no rational explanation for what is happening to this child.'

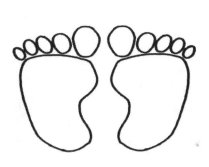

11

Before Liffey could turn the door knob, her phone vibrated for the third time. "Now what?" she barked impatiently into the phone.

"Is this Liffey Rivers?"

"Yes."

"This is Nurse Greene from ICU."

Liffey's heart began to beat rapidly. A feeling of dread began to creep over her.

Was Neil dead? Or dying? She did not think she could live without terrible guilt and sorrow for the rest of her life if he had given up his life to save hers.

"Please excuse my rude 'hello,' Nurse Greene. I am under a great deal of pressure at the moment."

"Yes. Well I can certainly understand stress."

"Do you have bad news?" Liffey could feel herself beginning to dissolve into a quivering blob.

"Quite the opposite, Liffey. Neil has not only returned to consciousness, he is moving his legs as well."

"Excuse me?" Liffey was not sure she understood what the ICU nurse had just told her.

"For lack of a better description, it is a miracle."

"May I visit him?"

"I thought you were on your way to Amsterdam at the moment?"

"As a matter of fact, there have been a few glitches since I left your hospital and it seems that am going to be in Johannesburg after all for a little while. My plane was cancelled."

"Well then, any taxi driver will know how to get here. As you know, you are only five minutes away."

Liffey was almost overcome with thankfulness. Neil was not going to die after all, and she just *knew* she could prove he was her brother.

"Thank you so much for the good news, Nurse Greene. I'll be right over after I finish up with some business here at the airport."

"May I tell Neil then that he can expect you?"

"Absolutely," Liffey answered.

"Thank you so much for the news."

***

The waiter in the non-descript Johannesburg café drew in a deep breath as he watched the odd French tourist leaving the restaurant, bobbing his head up and down like a bird pecking for worms in the ground.

'I need to find another job,' he thought. 'I can't take many more of these head cases losing it over their lunches.'

'Who does that guy think he is, Bird Man?'

***

Sam Snyder tried not to be too downcast. He knew Robert Rivers had good reason to be fed up with his sloppy surveillance of Liffey. Even though he suspected he was probably off the job now, he had Liffey's cell phone number and thought he would give her a call to see how she was doing.

He knew she had somehow stopped the man on the flight to Amsterdam but that was about all he knew. He wondered if there was anything he could do for her now.

***

Liffey began to turn the door knob for the fourth time when her cell phone vibrated like a small animal that was living in her pocket.

"Will this EVER stop?" she complained to Aunt Jean who was patiently waiting next to her in a floppy pink sunhat and matching pink sunglasses.

"Hello!"

"Hello, Liffey. This is Sam Snyder. Just checking up on you now that you are off the plane and probably in the terminal. Is there anything I can do for you before you board your next flight?"

Liffey wanted to yell, "Nooo!" but then looked once again at the fire alarm on the wall in front of her and this time noticed that it was different from any she had ever seen before.

Of course! She was in the airport security chief's *office*. This 'alarm' on the wall in here was not meant to be set off—it was a control panel, which would have monitoring devices. The system would be activated when a manual fire alarm was pulled somewhere in the airport, pinpointing the exact location where the alarm had been set off.

"Sam, I think I'm in trouble here. I am supposed to activate a fire alarm on the wall in front of me and then run for my life as usual, but it's not a real alarm box. It's like a map of all the alarms in the airport. It probably makes noise and flashes if an alarm goes off somewhere. Any ideas?"

'I need to think fast here,' Sam worried.

"Liffey, look around and see if there is some kind of loudspeaker paging system in the office? It would most

50

likely be on the main desk sitting next to, or be part of a PBX telephone console."

Liffey ran over to the biggest desk she could see in the unoccupied office and saw what looked like a microphone hooked up to a speaker next to a flat telephone with multiple buttons.

"Found it, Sam!"

"Great! All right then. Since you do not know how to operate it, go to your phone apps and see if you have anything like a siren. Then set it off and place your phone right next to the microphone on the desk. That should give you the results you want. I hope. Oh—and remember to take out your SIM card before you leave your phone next to the intercom microphone."

"And certainly remember to turn *on* the intercom! The siren alarm will keep sounding until somebody figures out what is happening or your phone charge wears off."

"Thanks so much, Sam. You may have just saved my life!"

Liffey found a loud, ear-splitting wake-up siren alarm on her phone. She turned toward her Aunt Jean to explain what they had to do next. "Aunt Jean. We are apparently in danger here and you need to help get us out of it. Turn the door knob when I say to and we will then run out into the hallway and head for the main entrance to the airport and calmly walk out. I am going to broadcast a fire alarm now."

"But Liffey! You will get into big trouble if you do that! You cannot continue acting out your fascination with fire alarms. It probably has to do with your fear of clowns and purging your bad memories of them, but I simply cannot allow this!"

"Okay, Aunt Jean. I guess you're right. We'll just leave quietly then. Would you please hold the door open for me?" Liffey asked politely as she pulled her SIM card from the phone and pressed the fire alarm wake-up app.

Before her aunt could forbid it again, Liffey switched on the loud speaker paging system, placed the phone directly next to the microphone and was thrilled when she heard loud, unsettling, honking sounds blasting in the hallway.

"We are so out of here right now, Aunt Jean!" Liffey cried. Yanking her aunt's arm and opening the door herself, she quickly moved both of them out of the office into the chaotic airport terminal's main lobby.

Liffey observed that most people were not behaving in an orderly fashion like the students at her old middle school had learned to do during fire drills. As the screaming siren blasted throughout the central airport concourse, it was obvious that nobody knew what the alarm meant.

Was there a bomb threat?

Fire alert?

Natural disaster?

The vast, multi-level terminal looked like a gigantic ant farm with swarming travelers all leaving at the same time.

The airport security officers, who had never heard that particular alarm before, looked confused and disoriented as Liffey, arm in arm with her aunt, briskly headed out of the main terminal door with hundreds of other travelers.

She immediately located the green limousine waiting in a reserved parking spot directly to the left of the main airport entrance.

"Come on Aunt Jean, they've sent this limo for us!"

"Who are 'they,' Liffey, and aren't we supposed to be getting on another flight to Amsterdam?"

"Not anymore, Aunt Jean."

"First, we are going to the hospital to see Neil who just woke up. Then, we are going to the U.S. Consulate office in Johannesburg."

"After that, I have no idea where we will be going."

Aunt Jean was too confused to say anything else as Liffey opened the limo door for her and gently pushed her inside.

She jumped in next to her aunt, slammed the door shut and the limo sped away.

"Hello, ladies," the driver said cheerfully.

"I trust you are enjoying your stay with us here in South Africa?"

12

It had not been easy for Liffey to persuade the driver of the black van and the super-sized bodyguards sent by the American Consulate to make a pit stop at the trauma center.

Liffey could tell right away after she had moved from the friendly green limo into the sinister-looking van, that she was going to get nowhere with her new escorts if she told them the real reason she wanted to stop at the hospital.

She said that she was experiencing heart palpitations and thought she had better be checked out at the nearest hospital.

This was partly true because she was so excited about seeing Neil again, she really could feel her heart fluttering in her chest.

Aunt Jean, who seemed to have forgotten all about Liffey's telling her that she wanted to visit Neil in the hospital, began to take over:

"Turn up the air conditioning, please, gentlemen. My niece needs oxygen." She placed an arm over Liffey's shoulder and gave her a reassuring squeeze.

"No wonder your poor little heart is beating out of control, Liffey, darling. How could one expect it not to be jumping around in your chest given all you have had to endure today?"

Liffey could see the driver's grim face in the rear view mirror. He did not appear to be at all sympathetic and was apparently checking to see if they were being followed.

Reluctantly, the consulate men agreed to stop at the hospital and turned off the Johannesburg route at the HOSPITAL sign.

When the van pulled up in front of the ER, Liffey jumped out and said she would be back as soon as she had her heart palpitations checked out.

Aunt Jean followed Liffey. The two guards shrugged and took up observation positions outside of the hospital. The driver remained in his seat looking tense and irritated.

Inside, Liffey darted past the ER entrance into the main hospital foyer and over to the elevators. She was astonished that her Aunt Jean had managed to keep up without being dragged along.

"Liffey, dear, don't you think we should stop at the ER first to have your heart examined?"

"Aunt Jean, my heart is fine. I just wanted to see Neil wiggling his toes before we go back to the States."

"But Liffey, Neil cannot move his legs so he would not be able to wiggle his toes."

"Something wonderful has happened to Neil, Aunt Jean. One of the calls I had at the airport before we left was from the head nurse in ICU. She told me that there has been some kind of miracle."

Before her aunt could continue this line of conversation, Liffey pulled the blonde wig from her head and handed it to her Aunt Jean who tucked it under her arm. When they reached the fifth floor, Liffey steered them toward Unit Four of the ICU.

Nurse Greene was sitting at her desk, talking on the phone and gestured at them to go in.

The crowd gathered in Unit Four looked like the happy ending scene from a family movie: A slight young boy in a hospital gown was sitting at the edge of his bed surrounded by doctors and nurses who appeared to be elated, yet guarded.

A nun dressed in a powder blue habit with a short white veil was standing in the far corner looking like she was having a mystical experience. She was weeping what Liffey supposed were tears of joy.

Liffey tiptoed into the unit and made her way over to the foot of the bed. At first Neil did not see her. When he finally felt her intense gaze, he turned his head and broke into a broad smile.

Liffey waved. He wiggled his toes back at her and grinned triumphantly.

The weeping nun blew her nose with a loud honk and looked at Liffey intently.

'Who *is* this young lady? She must be the American Irish dancer Neil had rescued.' Something about the natural way both of them were interacting now struck Sister Helen as unusual familiarity.

Neil was ordinarily painfully shy. Especially around girls. Yet here he was, totally relaxed and behaving like this girl was a long-lost best friend.

Sister Helen's train of thought jumped off the tracks and shifted dramatically. 'They have the same eyes and the same hair and the same porcelain skin and the same dimples,' she thought.

'I must be sleep deprived. This young lady is certainly not a relative. How could she be? What would the odds be that their paths could have crossed in such an unlikely way? And on another continent?'

'Yet I suppose that stranger things have happened…' Sister Helen made herself stop thinking along these lines.

Nurse Greene walked into the room and politely asked everyone who was not part of Neil's medical team to leave. Liffey edged over to the bed within earshot and gave him the victory sign. "I'll be in touch again soon, Neil." He smiled and returned the victory sign.

Realizing that she and her aunt had better be getting back to the U.S. Consulate van before the super-sized agents became impatient and started searching for her, Liffey reluctantly waved goodbye.

She hugged her aunt who had been watching from the doorway. Hand in hand, they set off down the long hospital corridor toward the elevators.

Inside the elevator, when Liffey pressed the 'Lobby' button, she began to feel queasy and a wave of pins and needles started running up and down her entire body on both sides. The prickling sensations stung and she tried not to cry out and alarm Aunt Jean, who was leaning peacefully against the elevator wall.

When they reached the lobby, Liffey said, "Aunt Jean, let's leave through the main entrance of the hospital and skip the walk through ER."

The lobby walls were almost entirely floor-to-ceiling tinted glass windows and Liffey had a clear view of the ER entrance off to their right.

A beautiful sunset was ushering in a purple twilight as Liffey tried to adjust her eyes to the growing darkness outside.

In the ER driveway, she could see that the black van was gone and there were no men in dark suits and sun glasses standing around the ER entrance looking ticked off. 'Where had they gone?'

Another wave of pins and needles began creeping across her forehead like a tight sweat band and Louise's warning at the airport came flying back into her tired head: "You cannot trust *anyone,* no matter who they are or say they are or seem to be."

"You cannot trust *anyone*, Liffey, do you understand?"

Could she trust her U.S. Consulate escort?

Before Liffey was able to determine whether or not the consulate van had ditched her and Aunt Jean, two white Gauteng police cars screeched to a halt in front of the ER where the van had been parked. Four uniformed officers jumped out of their vehicles and ran toward the hospital.

"Oh this is just great!" Liffey moaned under her breath.

"Come on, Aunt Jean, we need to go back upstairs."

Before Aunt Jean, who was becoming very sick of this day's events, could object, Liffey took her hand and speed-walked them over to the elevators. Luck was with them when one of the doors opened right away and Liffey pulled her aunt inside.

The doors opened again on the fifth floor where the weeping nun, who had been standing in the corner of Neil's ICU unit, was waiting to go down.

She was alone.

Liffey rushed out of the elevator, held the door open and pushed the #3 floor button, sending the elevator down before the startled nun could enter.

"Thank God you're here, Sister!" Liffey exclaimed.

"My aunt and I are in grave danger from the Gauteng Police and we need to hide from them immediately."

Liffey expected a barrage of skeptical questions from the nun. Instead, Sister Helen nodded gravely and motioned at them to follow her.

They walked rapidly past a large PEDIATRICS sign.

When they reached a busy central nursing station that looked more like a colorful play center with its bright beach murals and whale-shaped desks with built-in aquariums holding hundreds of tropical fish, Liffey saw what looked like an empty conference room.

Sister Helen instructed the nurses standing behind the whale desks that she was not to be disturbed and closed the conference room door behind Liffey and her aunt.

13

Nurse Greene marveled at the thin, earnest-looking nun walking by her desk wearing a light blue habit and white veil. She wore the same habit as Sister Helen's religious order but this nun did not look familiar.

The head nurse was certain that she had never seen this fervent nun before who was moving her lips, deep in prayer, as she pushed a young girl in a wheelchair past the ICU over to the 'Employees Only' elevator which went down to the cafeteria.

The pale young girl in the wheelchair looked frail in her oversized hospital gown and the dark circles under her eyes reminded Nurse Green of a raccoon. Long, braided pigtails lent a forlorn look to the sick girl's gaunt face.

The hospital encouraged personnel and volunteers to bring patients down to the cafeteria for 'outings' to break up the monotony of their long hospital stays. Many patients did not have family or friends available who were willing or able to transport them.

It was kind of this spirit-filled nun to volunteer to help out in the pediatric ward. 'I will have to introduce myself the next time I see her,' she thought. 'She certainly looks zealous. I cannot remember the last time I saw a sister walking along looking heavenward like that.'

***

Sister Helen had not worn street clothes since she had been in the novitiate. 'Thank heaven Jean was wearing sandals like me,' she thought. 'I would not in a million years have been able to pull off this clothing switch if I had to totter along in someone's high heels.'

Even though she had outfitted Jean in her own religious habit and was now wearing Jean's street clothes and Liffey's short blonde wig, she was somewhat fearful that someone in the hospital might recognize her since, in her capacity as head nurse at the Home for Disabled Children, she was on the pediatric staff here at the hospital.

Sister Helen left the break room in a white spaghetti strap sundress. The floppy pink sunhat Jean had been wearing had been stuffed into a large shopping bag with Liffey's green sweater, jeans and backpack. Fortunately, Jean had also been wearing a white, lightweight shrug which covered most of Sister Helen's thin, bare arms as she walked nonchalantly past Nurse Greene, making sure not to make eye contact.

When she reached the cafeteria, the plan was that she would station herself as a lookout at a table near the entrance.

Sister Helen did not know what to think about the wild stories featuring black mambas, international assassins and Saint Patrick's ancient snake bite cures that Liffey Rivers had briefed her about in the break room but she believed Liffey was telling the truth about the bizarre sequence of events today.

'Who on earth could possibly make up such tales? And as far as Liffey's hunch that Neil could be her blood brother? Why not?'

It was possible because Sister Helen knew that anything was possible in this life. She had learned long ago to follow her instincts if, combined with prayer, things felt 'right' to her. 'Who am I to doubt an old Sangoma woman who told Liffey that she and her "little brother were in the shadow of the serpent?" If Neil turns out to actually be her little brother, then both of them had indeed been in the shadow of the serpent.'

Prayerful reflection had led her to believe that first, she needed to follow Liffey's path and protect her from the dark forces pursuing her and second, she needed to do a sibling DNA test on Neil and Liffey.

In the break room, while they were switching wardrobes, she had laughed when Liffey had handed her a rootless, single hair from Neil's pillow.

"I am afraid that you watch too much television back home in the U.S.A., my dear," she said after Liffey had told her about how she had watched a forensic crime show in which a single hair provided DNA.

"You need at least five hairs with intact roots, Liffey, to get a reliable test result. But since I am on staff here at the hospital, I will get a test kit from the lab and do an inner cheek swab with a large Q-Tip on Neil while he's sleeping. As for you, stand still and open your mouth."

Sister Helen reached into a deep pocket of her habit and pulled out a large Q-Tip. She swiped the inside of Liffey's mouth on the right cheek and said, "There. Done."

She then placed the Q-Tip into a baggie she retrieved from another pocket. "I will have the results for you by the time you arrive back in the States."

***

'Sister Jean' had almost arrived at the elevator with the young girl in the wheelchair when she saw a woman with short blonde hair in a white sun dress signaling at her from down the hallway to hold the doors open.

All three entered the elevator and rode down in silence.

They parted company in the cafeteria. Sister Helen got herself a cup of coffee and a slice of cherry pie. She sat by herself near the entrance of the dining room.

'Sister Jean' parked Liffey at a table near the back of the cafeteria and returned with a large tray of assorted fruit and South African Klein River cheeses.

Liffey was starving. Since the greasy airport nachos, she had only had a few sips of bottled water. In spite of the fact that corrupt, or at the very least misinformed, local police were now chasing after her, she wanted to eat.

She began to cram cheese wedges into her mouth with both hands when 'Sister Jean' quietly pointed out, "Dear little one, you must not eat so enthusiastically or you might draw attention to yourself."

Aunt Jean had made a good point. 'I really should not be gobbling food now like a pig at a feeding trough.'

Liffey slowed down and began to nibble at her food like 'Sister Jean' had suggested.

Suddenly, a sensation of 'something is not right' blew in like a cold wind across the windowless cafeteria.

Liffey looked up and there they were.

As expected.

"It's show time, Sister," Liffey whispered, slumping back in her wheelchair.

'Sister Jean' leapt into action and began to act like a nurse. She held Liffey's wrist and pretended to take her pulse. Then she rearranged the thin blanket on Liffey's lap. The police had apparently split up for their search, as there were only two officers standing in the doorway.

One of the officers went over to interview Sister Helen who was pretending to be reading a newspaper while she ate her pie. 'Her hair looks good,' Liffey observed. 'Just like a regular pixie cut.'

Next, Liffey saw Sister Helen stand up and point out the door indicating, as they had rehearsed, that just before she came into the hospital, she had seen a young girl and a nervous looking woman getting into a taxicab outside of the main hospital entrance.

The police officer beckoned to his companion officer to join him and they both immediately left the cafeteria to pursue the escapees in the fictitious taxi.

Sister Helen sighed with relief and signaled for Liffey and 'Sister Jean' to join her. While she was eating her pie, she had thought of a way to help this young lady and her aunt to get out of South Africa safely, and she would not even have to make a phone call.

Liffey was able to stuff three more pieces of cheese into her mouth before her wheelchair began to move out.

***

The law office's corporate jet began a slow descent as it approached Chicago Rockford International Airport space.

There still had been no word from Liffey or Jean since they had been instructed to leave Oliver Tambo Airport. According to Sam, Liffey's phone was now out of commission because she had removed her SIM card when she activated a phone siren alarm application. Calls to Jean went directly to her voice mail.

Robert Rivers tried to remain calm. Now that Maeve seemed to be making giant steps in recovering her memory and normal social skills, he did not want to upset her with his fears concerning Liffey and his sister.

Louise had told him that she had instructed Liffey to activate a fire alarm and immediately clear out of Oliver Tambo Airport because she suspected that Liffey's security had been compromised. Louise had heard nothing yet from

Liffey regarding her escape from the airport. However, earlier in the day, she had learned that there had been a mass evacuation at Oliver Tambo's International Passenger Terminal.

His last communication with Louise more than an hour ago had been dreadful: "Robert, as you know, I arranged protective custody for Liffey and Jean with the U.S. Consulate in Johannesburg. They just called to report that the agents who had been dispatched to pick up Liffey and Jean at an airport exit are missing. They have not checked in since they confirmed picking up Liffey and your sister."

✳✳✳

The Raven was playing solitaire, trying to unwind on the new eucalyptus wood deck he had installed in back of his modest residence just outside of the Johannesburg city limits.

Tomorrow he would return to his real home on his private game reserve and regroup. He would shoot a few animals and try to relax.

His nerves and patience were gone. He was ashamed that the waiter earlier today in the Johannesburg café had witnessed what his mother had always referred to as one of his "bird fits."

14

Helen watched the hallway until the two Gauteng police officers disappeared around a corner. She had a plan.

"Walk casually out to the car park with me, ladies, to my vehicle. If anyone is watching us, it will look very normal placing Liffey on the van's wheelchair lift accompanied by one of the nuns from the Home."

When Liffey had been lifted up into the aging blue van, Sister Helen informed them that their next stop would be the private charter terminal at Oliver Tambo Airport where Liffey and Jean would board a medical pilgrimage plane leaving in a few hours for the Marian shrine in Lourdes, France.

"I organized this year's diocesan trip for the sick and infirm along with many volunteers to assist them. There is no one who will question me when I present your passports and personally accompany both of you on to the plane."

"I will explain that the two of you have taken Neil's and my places. After all the media coverage about the snake today, no one will expect the two of us to be going. Which reminds me, 'Sister Jean,' we need to switch back into the same clothes we put on this morning when we began this remarkable day."

"You mean I am going to Lourdes in this wheelchair?"

"Yes, dear. You and your aunt are going to be pilgrims. We need to get you back into your own clothes too since you are hardly dressed for a transcontinental flight in that flimsy hospital gown."

After they had switched back into their original clothing, sister Helen elaborated, "I will tell the tour guide in charge that you missed your flight to Lourdes and will be meeting up with another pilgrimage group in France. This will spare you from having to sneak away from my group when you arrive at the airport. You will then book the first flight to Charles De Gaulle Airport in Paris that you can get. Then, when you get to Paris, buy tickets to any place in the United States—except Chicago."

"The corrupt police, or perhaps that demonic man who never seems to stop pursuing you, may have ways to discover that you are on a flight to Chicago. They probably would expect that. So go anywhere else first."

"I will be praying for you with my fellow sisters for protection and guidance. In the meantime, please call your poor father before he has a heart attack from worry—here's my mobile."

Liffey was amazed. It seemed that Sister Helen had thought of everything. The identity switch with Aunt Jean in the break room, putting Liffey in a wheelchair, and now, escaping from South Africa as a pilgrim on her way to Lourdes, France.

'This awesome nun has figured out a way to get me out of here and I believe that it is actually going to work,' she thought hopefully.

Even Aunt Jean thought it was an "exciting" idea and was already worrying about the proper dress attire for a pilgrimage.

"I have never been on a religious pilgrimage before, Sister Helen. What does one wear if one is not a nun?"

***

When Liffey finally managed to call Robert Rivers from Sister Helen's mobile phone and told him she was about to board a chartered flight to France, he looked like he had come back from the dead. The color returned to his face and he radiated relief and happiness.

"I will work out your itinerary from Paris, Liffey. Go to the Air France desk when you get there to collect your tickets. After that, buy a cheap mobile phone in a shop and get back to me with your number. I can't get through on Jean's phone. Sister Helen is right about your not coming into Chicago. New York would be good. I'll call Louise in Boston and have her get in touch with you about meeting up in New York tomorrow. Thank God, we'll be seeing you soon then."

Attorney Rivers turned around and said, "Okay, ladies, I say we all get off this plane right now and find some chili!"

Maeve agreed enthusiastically.

Sinead tried to mask the fact that she would rather eat dirt and agreed that it was a wonderful idea.

***

Robert Rivers drove slowly along the little-traveled back country road shortcuts from Illinois to Wisconsin. Both of his passengers had fallen asleep shortly after eating a bowl of Tailgate Chili at his favorite truck stop restaurant on the interstate.

His mind wandered back to a small room in Ireland at Sligo General Hospital, where the dim green night lights

68

had cast an eerie glow over Maeve McDermott Rivers as she slept fitfully in her world of dreams.

Whenever Maeve had said anything in Sligo, it usually sounded like gibberish. Even though it seemed hopeless, Attorney Rivers had recorded every word she said, hoping some of them might provide a clue as to some of the places she had been for the past ten years.

At the end of each day, he sent Maeve's recorded words to his staff of investigators in Chicago. They made copies, then forwarded the recordings on to a group of forensic translation experts for deciphering.

His staff had informed him that the experts were fairly certain that the recurring words Maeve blurted out most often were of West African origin. They had said that, "Repetitive words sounding like 'men-dee' and 'boon-doo' were probably from the Bundu people who were a branch of the Mende nation in West Africa."

It was entirely possible that Maeve had ended up on the west coast of Africa when her plane went missing. Robert Rivers was becoming more and more convinced that his wife had been removed like baggage from her medical transport carrier en route to Switzerland and then left behind to rot on a jungle runway.

After her plane took off without her, it had exploded mid-air near the Canary Islands.

That seemed to be the only possible explanation for Maeve's miraculous reappearance. Her plane must have been hijacked before it had discarded her. He had no theory yet as to how her terminal cancer had been reversed and general good health, with the exception of her amnesia, restored.

Considering what he *did* know about Maeve's life during the past ten years, that she had developed amnesia and worked unknowingly with a dangerous diamond smuggler who told her that he was her brother, it made sense that her medical transport plane had been forced to land on Africa's west coast where illicit diamonds were routinely smuggled out of Africa.

Her flight had disappeared twice off radar. Once for approximately thirty minutes, the time it would have taken to land the plane, pick up illegal diamonds and leave Maeve behind in the jungle.

The second time the plane went off radar, it never re-appeared. When pieces of a small plane washed up on a beach in the Canary Islands days later, it was obvious that the plane had blown up.

After they were settled in, he would begin the process of trying to pinpoint the exact area of West Africa where Maeve's plane had gone off radar the first time.

By far the most unsettling discovery concerning Maeve's past, was the fact that the doctors in Ireland had discovered a tiny C-section birth scar on her abdomen.

Liffey's delivery had been uncomplicated. There had been no C-section. No birth scar.

If this were a court case, he would tell the jury that there was "compelling evidence" that Maeve McDermott Rivers had given birth to another child.

But that was impossible. Maeve had been dying when they had discovered she was expecting another child.

But she did not die.

So maybe their child had not died either.

Attorney Rivers tried not to consider the possibility that there was a child of his missing somewhere out there. It was too much to bear.

'One day at a time,' he thought. 'That's all I can manage.'

***

Sinead was amazed at how huge Liffey's split-level house was. She stood in the entrance hallway and gaped. 'This place has got to be bigger than Dublin Castle,' she thought. 'Liffey never mentioned that she lived in a palace.'

Maeve Rivers looked around the premises with a strange expression on her face and said, "Robert, this place looks very familiar." He tried not to show how elated he was that Maeve's memory seemed to be returning in bits and pieces like Dr. Morrow in Sligo said it might.

Before Robert Rivers, who was now fumbling for words having this discussion, could answer, a small terrier came running toward him from the kitchen.

The barking dog was followed by Lewis, the house and dog sitter the Rivers family hired whenever they were going to be out of town for more than a long weekend. Lewis announced that there had been no problems and Max had behaved well.

"What a precious little dog, Robert!"

"This is Max the Magnificent, Maeve."

"You two have not met before. Liffey and I got him after…"

"After I was gone, Robert?"

"Yes. After you were gone."

Sinead had heard Liffey tell many stories about her dog, Max. "Is it true, Mr. Rivers, that Max attacked a blue clown in church once and Liffey had to pull him off the clown's ankle?"

Robert Rivers looked perplexed and Sinead hoped she had not said something that was going to get Liffey in trouble later. There were probably many stories Liffey had told her but not 'shared' with her father.

Maeve walked into the living room and then went on to the kitchen followed by Max who was frantically sniffing her shoes. She returned shortly with an inquiry, "Robert, why is there no furniture in the dining room?"

Sinead could see the confused look on Robert Rivers' face.

"Mr. Rivers, I believe Liffey told me some time ago that her aunt wanted to use the nice wooden floor in your dining room for practicing their Irish dancing steps. She said her aunt said that all the furniture had to go so something called 'feng shui' could happen to allow positive energy to flow through the room."

Before Sinead had to answer any of the angry follow-up questions she could see brewing in Mr. Rivers' head, her own head began to throb and she felt sick to her stomach.

"Excuse me, please, I think I am going to be sick!"

Maeve, who had been trying not to laugh at Robert Rivers trying to control the look of outrage on his face after he had discovered his sister's house 'remodeling,' led Sinead to the closest bathroom and waited politely outside.

"Mrs. Rivers, I think I need to lie down," Sinead said after she had been sick. She was noticeably limping as she walked from the bathroom to the guest bedroom.

"Of course, Sinead. Right away, dear. I could tell that the spicy chili dinner we ate on the way home from the airport did not seem to agree with you. I should never have suggested you have that apple pie for dessert when you already looked a bit green. You need to get some proper rest. Liffey will be here tomorrow night and then you two will probably not sleep for weeks! The day after tomorrow is New Year's Eve. We'll have to be sure to call your family."

Maeve put her arm around Sinead's waist and helped her into the largest of two spacious guest rooms overlooking Delavan Lake which was shrouded in early evening gloom.

"Thank you for being so kind to me in Ireland, Sinead. I am so very happy that you came back with us for a visit. Liffey is going to be so surprised to find you here!"

Maeve fluffed the pillows and walked over to the sliding glass door where Sinead stood gazing out at the lake's tranquil, dark water. Sinead smiled feebly and asked, "Mrs. Rivers, is that mournful sound coming from off the lake a loon? I read all about them when I was reading about Wisconsin water birds."

Maeve listened carefully and answered, "I don't hear anything, Sinead. But whatever you are hearing, it can't be a loon. Loons migrate south to the Gulf Coast from Wisconsin when it starts to get cold. And to be honest, most loons live up in Northern Wisconsin. Even in the summer."

It was not until after Maeve returned to the living room after settling Sinead into a guest bedroom that she realized she had remembered exactly where the nearest bathroom to the house entrance was located and after that, where the two guest rooms were situated overlooking the lake.

Her memory was coming back.

15

*A*unt Jean had been so impressed with the invalids and volunteers and overall devout atmosphere on the charter flight to Lourdes that she suggested to Liffey that they continue on to the famous Marian shrine with the group.

"I think that I would like to explore becoming a nun, Liffey. I have been thinking about it for hours now."

Liffey patiently reminded her aunt that they were hardly out of the woods yet and that they both needed to get back to the States where they would be much safer.

"Besides, Aunt Jean," Liffey told her newly converted aunt, "until today you had never even mentioned going on a pilgrimage anywhere."

"And I can't even remember the last time you wanted to go to Mass with me on Sunday."

"That is a good point, Liffey. If I am going to become a nun, I suppose I really should start going to church on Sundays. We will plan another religious experience around a feis at a more convenient time. If we can find one in Rome, perhaps we could meet up with the Pope to discuss my vocation to the sisterhood."

By the time their early afternoon flight from Paris on Air France had arrived in New York eight hours later, Aunt Jean had forgotten all about being holy.

She had watched *Project Runway* reruns for five hours on the plane before Liffey suggested that she take a nap. Now that her aunt's religious fervor had subsided, she was plotting a trip back to Paris for next spring's fashion week.

***

As instructed by Louise, after they had cleared customs in New York, they walked out into the exit area where they were greeted by a man holding a MILLER FAMILY sign who escorted them outside into an off duty taxi.

"I cannot imagine why Louise told this man we were the *Miller* family, Liffey."

"I am guessing it might be because she did not think it was a good idea to announce the arrival of the *Rivers* family, Aunt Jean. We have kind of been on the run lately in case you haven't noticed," Liffey said, trying not to sound overly sarcastic.

The cab drove them to a small airport in New Jersey where they were met by Louise at the front entrance of the general aviation area.

Liffey was so happy to see Louise that she could hardly contain herself and hugged her detective friend hard like she used to hold on to her father's waist when they went downhill sledding.

Louise smiled broadly and said, "We'll visit on the plane, ladies. Sam called and told me he found out that someone had run an unauthorized computer check of international flights arriving in the U.S. from South Africa, so it's a good thing that Sister Helen lady thought to send you out of the country on a private charter flight to France."

"Even if anyone *had* thought to check all the private charters to Europe from South Africa, Louise, they would not have turned up our names on a passenger manifest because Sister Helen left hers and Neil's reservations on the list."

"Sister Helen is a remarkable lady," Louise said.

Liffey was surprised when, after Louise had escorted them over to a small turboprop plane sitting inside of a remote private plane hanger, she plopped down in the pilot's seat.

"Didn't know I was a pilot, did you, Liffey?"

"No," Liffey admitted, "this is very cool!"

Aunt Jean agreed and asked if she could be the co-pilot.

Liffey smiled, shook her head and settled back into one of the four comfortable passenger seats.

Louise reached under her seat and handed Liffey and her aunt two warm boxes of Chinese takeout food labeled 'Shrimp Fried Rice' along with two bottles of ice tea.

"Congratulations. Both of you deserve a combat medal for bravery," Louise said ceremoniously, "but all I've got is your favorite food, Liffey."

Liffey was ecstatic. "Thanks, Louise, I'm starving!"

After she had devoured every kernel of rice, she sleepily buckled her seatbelt and tried to keep her eyes open.

***

It was barely light outside when Louise got clearance to take off but Liffey could still see a line of golden sunset looming far off in the western winter sky as the plane climbed and headed west.

'I have been on three continents in the last twenty-four hours,' Liffey thought sleepily, trying to stay awake.

While Louise was complaining about the prevailing winds working against their plane's making good time flying from Eastern Standard Time into Central Standard Time,

Liffey was wondering what time it was in France, and South Africa, and Amsterdam, and Wisconsin, before she closed her eyes, finally permitting sleep to come over her.

She was safe.

At least for the time being.

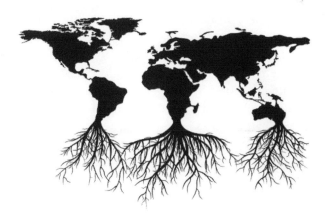

16

Sister Helen returned to the ICU unit early the next morning and was ecstatic when she learned that Neil had been moved to a less critical patient area.

He was sleeping comfortably when she gently swabbed the inside of his mouth on the left side.

She went to the head nurse's station and read his chart. It indicated that his vital signs were all within normal ranges and that he continued to move his 'paralyzed' legs.

Other than being extremely weak, he showed no signs of distress. It was nothing less than a miracle.

She made a mental note to ask Liffey Rivers to explain in greater detail her interesting theory that Saint Patrick might have had something to do with Neil's miraculous recovery—something about pages of a book being taken out of Ireland and then shredded and mixed with Gatorade.

***

Police Superintendant Johnson picked up his mobile phone and saw that there was another missed call from Monsieur Poinsette.

He could no longer avoid telling Monsieur the bad news. He dialed his phone, hoping there would be no answer and that he would be able to leave voice mail but Monsieur Poinsette picked up on the first ring.

"I regret to tell you that we have been unsuccessful in assisting you with your search for the American girl and her aunt. There is no record of them having left Johannesburg from Oliver Tambo in the last twenty-four hours and none of my officers have been able to pick up their trail."

"I am afraid they have completely vanished, Monsieur Poinsette."

The Raven disconnected the call without commenting on the bad news he had just received.

"Idiots," he raged aloud. "How hard can it be to flush out a few American tourists?"

"When my cast is off and I can use my right arm again, I will put an end to this ongoing nightmare myself. There will be no more failed attempts."

***

Detective Steve Powers had been sleeping in the Intensive Care Unit ever since he had been transported there from Oliver Tambo Airport in a coma.

He woke up briefly and saw that next to him, on a flimsy gray tray stand, there was a large floral arrangement of blue carnations. The card next to it said: "Get Well Soon! We miss you!"

It was signed by his co-workers at Legal Investigations, Ltd.

His head felt like it was being stretched across the room like a rubber band. Try as he could, he could not remember how he got here. He closed his eyes again and fell back into a deep sleep.

***

'De Slang' was in the Central Prison Hospital in Pretoria in critical condition. It was hoped that he would pull through and unmask other 'persons of interest' to international policing agencies. But his prognosis was poor, as venom from a black mamba snake had entered his body through a needle injection in his neck. 'The Snake' was not expected to live.

***

Sam Snyder decided it was time to grab some significant sleep before he traveled to Wisconsin from Illinois to pick up the Rivers ladies at a landing strip in Walworth County.

After he had collected them, he would return to his surveillance post and watch their lake house from the bushes across the street. He would have to stop for some Oreo cookies if he was going to have any staying power through the night.

***

The three U.S. Consulate workers in Johannesburg, South Africa, eventually managed to untie themselves and crawled out from the ditch where their abductors had left them along an isolated back road not far from Oliver Tambo Airport. Their mobile phones and wallets had been stolen, along with most of their outer clothing and dignity, after they had been taken at gunpoint outside the hospital.

They had no idea what had become of their charges, Liffey Rivers and her aunt.

***

When Maeve Rivers went to check on Sinead McGowan for the fifth time, she was dismayed to see Sinead was still sound asleep.

It was 3:00 p.m. and even if Sinead was suffering from extreme jet lag, she ought to have been up at least once by now since she had gone to bed so early the night before.

"Something is not right with that girl, Robert," Maeve insisted.

"I had noticed in Sligo that Sinead was acting peculiarly and she was also very pale," Robert said.

"I thought that if she continued to look so under-the-weather after we got her back here, we could take her to our family doctor, June Root."

"You've never met her but I've been very pleased with her over the years. Tomorrow night is New Year's Eve. I'll give Dr. Root's office a call right now and see if they can work her in immediately after the holiday."

"I'm not sure it can wait that long, Robert. I have a bad feeling... Sinead looks like she's at death's door. And a crow has been sitting on a branch outside her window all day."

"Oh for heaven's sake, Maeve. Surely you don't believe that old Irish superstition that the crow is a harbinger of death?"

"I don't know what I believe, Robert, but the day my grandmother died, a crow sat on her window sill all day long, looking in at her. I saw it."

"If Sinead has not significantly improved by the time Liffey and Jean arrive, I am going to call her parents in Sligo and tell them we are bringing her to the hospital."

17

L ouise deftly landed the Cessna on a private, lighted runway located in a housing community not far from the Illinois-Wisconsin border. It was owned and operated by a group of professional airline pilots who lived in rural Wisconsin and commuted to Chicago airports when they reported to their airlines for flight assignments.

Aunt Jean watched Louise and then pretended to be working the co-pilot instruments as their plane landed. She reminded Liffey of a three-year-old steering a car while sitting on her parent's lap.

Louise was grateful when Sam Snyder had called and confirmed that he would pick up Liffey and Jean and drive them home while she refueled and went back to Saint Louis. 'This assignment will never end,' she thought. 'I'm just about completely done in.'

***

Liffey was well aware that she owed everyone a major apology for sneaking off to South Africa with Aunt Jean after the feis in New York and not telling anyone what she was up to.

Of course, if she *had* told anyone, her father would have found out and forbidden her to go and then she would have never met her brother. It was hard to think coherently lately as she had been traveling over three continents since yesterday, and was completely burnt-out.

In the car, Liffey tried to explain: "Happy New Year, a bit early, Sam, and thank you so much for saving my life at the airport!"

Liffey noticed Louise giving Sam a perplexed look and explained, "If Sam had not called me in the office at Oliver Tambo when I was trying to figure out the fire alarm system, I might not be here now. He told me what to do and how to do it and it worked great!"

"I hope picking us up now isn't messing up any holiday travel plans you have, Sam, and I am *really* sorry I've caused everyone so much trouble. I never meant for anyone to go through all this. I honestly thought Aunt Jean and I would be off to Africa and back again before anyone noticed."

'Noticed?' Sam bit his tongue.

'I suppose that Liffey really has no idea that she has been under twenty-four hours a day surveillance since she returned from Ireland,' he thought. 'In her mind, she was just extending her New York feis time. I am certain that Attorney Rivers never told Liffey she was being tailed by his staff detectives. Why else would I be spending my time hiding in the bushes outside of her house?'

'However, I would be willing to bet that Liffey and her aunt were under orders to tell Attorney Rivers if they were ever planning to leave town.'

"No need for apologies, Liffey. All of us are just very grateful you made it back in one piece," Sam said.

'Almost one piece,' Liffey thought. A big piece of her remained in South Africa in a hospital bed.

Liffey picked up the cheap phone she had purchased in France, breathed in and dialed Sister Helen. It was an easy number: 27 011-God-Love. It would be almost dawn now in South Africa. She would leave voice mail for Sister Helen if she did not answer.

***

Sister Helen had not been shocked at the results of the DNA swab tests. The first time she had looked into Liffey Rivers' eyes she had seen what many religious vocation types like herself might call a 'seer,' someone who has knowledge or insight coming from a spiritual place that most people did not know how to dial up on demand.

The swab test had confirmed that Liffey and Neil were brother and sister—something that Liffey Rivers somehow already knew. This could be great news for Neil. Sister Helen was aware that he was lonely and fairly isolated at the Home. But she had no idea how she would be able to cope with Neil leaving her before he was at least sixteen.

She had always known he would grow up someday and go out into the world and had worked with him since he was four years old to make sure that his proficiency in multiple languages and math and science was superior.

She would certainly not tell Neil that Liffey Rivers was his sister, not before she interviewed Liffey's father first as to what, if any, intentions he might have regarding his son.

Liffey had assured her that Robert Rivers had no idea that his child had been born after his wife went missing. Even so, she was not about to put Neil in a frame of mind which might lead him to believe he was going to be reunited with his birth family if this was not likely to happen. And she had to make sure that Liffey's father was the honorable, good man, Liffey had assured her he was, prior to even considering the possibility of his leaving South Africa.

She had legal custody of Neil. Or at least the Holy Childhood Sisters did. In the end, she knew she would do what would be in Neil's best interests. No matter if it would break her own heart.

***

Sister Helen hesitantly answered her phone. After a short conversation with Liffey Rivers, she closed her eyes and prayed, "God, please give me strength."

***

Liffey felt numb. She was thrilled with the confirmation from Sister Helen that Neil was her brother but she was also jittery and somewhat frightened.

How was she going to bring up this subject with her father?

What if Neil did not want to come and live with her family?

He might not.

Would they then have to force him?

They would never do that.

That would be terrible.

What if her mother never remembered she had given birth to a baby boy?

'She might not even remember *my* birth,' Liffey thought glumly.

'Maybe this was not such a great idea after all.'

18

Sinead woke up headache free at 9:00 p.m. and was ravenously hungry. 'Mrs. Rivers was so happy to see me eating this chicken noodle soup it was weird,' she reflected, spooning the last drop of broth out of her bowl.

According to Robert Rivers, Liffey had called from the New Jersey airport just before her small plane took off, so that meant she should be arriving any time now. The plan was not to mention that Sinead was already there and let Liffey discover her watching television in the corner of the large living room.

Maeve Rivers was resting and Robert Rivers was pacing around the house like a palace guard expecting an attack.

'I hope Mr. Rivers calms down and isn't quite so high strung after Liffey gets here. He keeps looking at me like something is wrong with me and it's making me nervous.'

***

Sam Snyder drove down the long driveway past the small yellow stucco gatehouse that Liffey had used as a playhouse when she was little.

Liffey tried hard to envision herself walking through the front door to her house with her mother waiting for her inside, but she could not. This was all very overwhelming and Liffey needed some more time to try to process all of the new family relationship dynamics she was about to be clobbered with.

She needed to talk to Sinead for some moral support before she could face walking through the door. Even though Liffey knew Sinead would never be up so early, she dialed anyway.

"Hello there, Liffey! Are you back in the States yet? I am desperate to hear all about everything over here in County Dull, Ireland."

"Sinead, I am freaking out! I'm finally at my own front door all safe and sound but I am just as scared as I was when the black mamba popped out of that picnic basket."

"Liffey, cheer up! You'll see. It'll be all natural-like and in no time it will feel like your mum never left you."

"Yeah. Sure. Okay. Great. I'll call you later then," Liffey said impatiently when it was obvious that Sinead was not going to be any help sorting things out.

"*Please* don't forget to call me later, Liffey. I want to hear all about Africa," Sinead begged.

Aunt Jean opened the door for Liffey, who was toting their two carryon bags.

"Don't you worry, Liffey, darling. I am sure that our real luggage will turn up soon and you will be able to wear your new safari solo dress at the Winter Feis."

Liffey cringed. 'That might be the only positive thing about losing all of our luggage,' she thought.

Sam Snyder drove off, delaying the inevitable face-to-face confrontation with his employer until after the new year.

Before Liffey could enter, the door opened and she was embraced warmly by Maeve Rivers in the doorway.

"Welcome home, Liffey." She hugged Liffey close and suddenly it seemed as if the ten years of her mother's absence had only been ten minutes. The ache was gone and there were going to be lilacs next May that she would enjoy again with her *mother* in the backyard. Liffey had not felt as safe as this for as long as she could remember.

Aunt Jean tiptoed around them and looked sheepishly around the corner for her brother, Robert, who, as Liffey had pointed out on the plane, might be so angry with both of them that they had better not speak until spoken to.

Jean also needed to discuss the concept of 'feng shui' with Robert which would explain the absence of his dining room furniture.

Arm in arm, Maeve walked Liffey into the living room. "Have you talked to Sinead lately, Liffey?"

"Yes. As a matter of fact, I called her just outside the front door."

Sinead could not stand the suspense any longer and before Liffey had discovered that she was sitting just twenty feet away, she jumped up from the couch and shouted: "Surprise!"

Liffey had no time to react as Sinead raced towards her with outstretched arms. She had almost reached Liffey, when, instead of hugging her shocked friend, she suddenly stopped, grabbed her own head with both hands, cried out in pain and slumped down to the floor.

"Robert, should we call 911?"

Maeve already had a phone in her hands.

"Let's get her in bed first and see if she comes right back. Sinead is a very emotional girl and it's possible she is just overcome with all this excitement."

Robert Rivers scooped Sinead up in his arms and carried her carefully into the guest room followed by Maeve and Liffey and Max.

As he had predicted, when they had arranged Sinead in bed, she immediately opened her eyes and said, "Well now, how's that for an early New Year's stunt?"

Liffey laughed. She loved Sinead's quick wit even though sometimes her jokes were so lame they made her groan.

"How did you not tell me you were up to this? I would never have been able to keep it secret!" Liffey said.

Sinead opened her mouth to reply but was cut off by the saddest howling Liffey had ever heard. It seemed to be coming from the direction of the lake.

A shudder went through the room. Maeve's eyes looked like they were too big for their sockets and were about to pop out.

Aunt Jean came rushing in.

"Did you hear that awful wailing noise coming from the lake? It sounds like an animal might be caught in a trap!"

"Or coyotes? They make a terrible racket. Make sure none of you accidentally allows Max outside or he'll be their late night snack," Robert Rivers said.

Aunt Jean was about to go on when Sinead cut in.

"It's not an animal out there. It's the O'Neill Banshee," she whispered hoarsely.

Liffey and her mother exchanged worried glances.

"My mother is an O'Neill," Sinead continued, "and she heard it once when it was wailing outside her grandfather's window, warning everyone that he was about to pass over."

"Now, it's come to warn me, but I already know."

A profound stillness crept slowly over the room, like the complete silence that comes just before a storm when all the birds stop chirping.

There was only a dismal keening coming from the lake.

19

L iffey Rivers and her mother, Maeve, sat next to Sinead McGowan's parents in the University of Wisconsin Hospital's Neurosurgery waiting room.

The doctors had explained that Sinead's aggressive brain tumor should have been removed weeks before she had collapsed.

Mrs. McGowan was inconsolable. "How could I not have known what was going on? All those headaches but never letting on how sick she was because she so wanted to come to the States."

Robert Rivers stopped pacing around the room.

"How can *any* parent know what their child is really up to?" He flashed a directional look at Liffey.

"Daddy, I swear I never had any idea Sinead was sick! She never said anything about it."

"I know that, Liffey," he replied gently. "It's just such a tragedy. Her walking around for weeks crashing into things and popping pills every four hours. I believed her when she told me she had a nasty sinus condition."

"And how in the world could I not have seen that those bizarre episodes of weeping about how baby cuckoo birds were going to murder baby Irish birds in the spring were—just cuckoo!" Mrs. McGowan added.

"So that's where Sinead's cheesy sense of humor gene comes from," Liffey smiled.

"I dismissed her bizarre behavior as being a case of imbalanced hormones," Mrs. McGowan continued.

"Her brothers tried to tell me they thought she was hiding something and acting peculiarly but I didn't listen. And now…"

"And now, here we all are! Right where Sinead is supposed to be—in one of the best hospitals, with one of the best neurosurgeons in the United States looking after her, and her family and friends by her side."

Liffey exhaled. It was *so* nice having a mother around to say on-point things like that.

***

Breda and Joseph McGowan returned to Ireland three weeks after Sinead's surgery, when it was clear that their daughter was recovering and well on her way back to her normal self again. The outdoor lambing season on their three hundred acre sheep farm would begin in late February and each year it was touch and go for many of the newborn lambs.

Sinead explained that her parents needed to vaccinate the expectant ewes four to six weeks before the lambs came and then organize the nutritional management of all their expectant mothers. "Try to imagine supervising the births of hundreds of lambs over a period of only a few weeks!"

Sinead said that her parents did ultrasound studies on the ewes to see if they were going to deliver one, two or sometimes three lambs. Then the sheep were separated into groups to prepare for any possible assistance that they might require delivering their babies.

Since Sinead was under doctor's orders not to travel during her recovery, especially by plane, it was decided that she would remain with the Rivers until her doctors said she could return to Ireland.

Sheila Sullivan, the private duty nurse Mr. Rivers had already hired to care for his wife, moved into the estate gate house. Since Maeve was doing so well, Sheila Sullivan's primary concern would be observing Sinead for any signs of seizures or problems with speech or coordination.

***

Aunt Jean came two days each week to teach her 'School of Life' methods in spite of the fact that her brother had hired a professional 'robot,' as Liffey referred to the tutor, who came three days a week to supervise the girls' academic progress.

"Your aunt is so cool, Liffey. It's like we are not really studying anything at all."

"Unfortunately, that's the way daddy looks at it too, Sinead." Liffey bit her bottom lip. "We totally have to get both of us out of this house soon. It's almost May and I am sick of walking you around the grounds like I'm exercising Max."

Sinead laughed. "Well, Liffey, I am thinking it won't be much longer at all. Dr. Root confers with the Madison doctors every two weeks and everybody seems to think I am doing remarkably well, soooo…."

"So then. I'll get to work on something big," Liffey said.

***

Liffey was somewhat ashamed of herself for being so impatient about everything. Even though some of her mother's memory had returned, she was not allowed to drive because of her serious head injury up on Knocknarea, and she usually slept almost fifteen hours a day. Liffey felt like she had not made much progress in getting to know her mother again. They would be having a very interesting conversation and then, right in the middle of it, Maeve would get so weak she had to go and lie down.

Also, she desperately needed to tell her father about her brother, Neil, in South Africa.

Sister Helen had asked her to wait until he was making more progress with his legs. She said he was able to stand up now and take a few steps with a walker. Since his leg muscles were so atrophied, he had physical therapy twice a day.

Sister Helen thought it best for Neil not to know about "things" until he was on his feet more. He needed all his energy right then to work on strengthening his leg muscles.

When Liffey had asked Sister Helen to explain how this miraculous reverse paralysis thing could have happened, she tried to explain: "There is snake venom research going on all over the world now. Researchers have discovered that compounds in some snake venoms which are normally lethal, may also be developed to actually help to repair human bodies and even fight disease."

"Last week I read that so much progress has been made with using the proteins in snake venom in one therapy or another, that now, for every single person who dies from snake bite, three hundred and fifty people are helped."

Liffey had reluctantly agreed to respect Sister Helen's wishes and sent Neil greeting cards with notes and photos twice a week, promising to visit as soon as she could.

When the dining room furniture was returned, the room lost its 'feng shui' as Aunt Jean had predicted, and Maeve switched Irish dance practices to the basement, where she installed a proper floor and drilled Liffey and Sinead several times a week.

In the meantime, Aunt Jean was Liffey's only means of getting away because her father was so busy doing long delayed trials in Chicago, making up for the months he had spent in Ireland with her mother, that she hardly ever saw him.

Aunt Jean drove her to Irish dance lessons in Milwaukee once a week but Liffey's teachers still ignored her. Even though she was now in Open in her Jig and Hornpipe, they did not teach her any Open Prizewinner steps.

So Liffey concentrated on planning a cruise. 'Maybe if I suggest that we plan an Alaskan cruise with Sinead, Aunt Jean and mother, it could actually happen,' she hoped.

'The doctors can't keep Sinead locked up here forever and we haven't done anything fun since she got here. Plus, daddy feels guilty about being away so much and all of us being so cooped up here. This could work.'

Liffey texted her Aunt Jean with the cruise idea and had a reply in less than two minutes:

"Absolutely! U handle RR. I will do rest. A.J."

***

Sam Snyder watched the Rivers' estate from the dense bushes across the street.

At least it was another day shift and he might get in some 'following his client around' time. He was fed up just sitting there day after day eating Oreos during his eight hour shifts, trying to stay awake.

Liffey's Aunt Jean drove her to Irish dance class in Milwaukee once a week and tailing them both ways was some diversion, but not much.

'Soon, I am going to request client intake at the office assignments,' he thought.

Rumor had it that Robert Rivers had just hired another investigator, so now would be a logical time to beg off this assignment—at least for a few months.

"Let that new guy sit here all day. I need a break," he griped, cramming another Oreo cookie into his mouth and chugging down the remainder of his carton of milk.

Two other law office investigators took the other shifts in rotation, but Sam had had enough fooling around with surveillance equipment, watching for intruders.

Except for the snake incident a few months ago, it had become a very boring routine.

'If someone was going to try another hit on Liffey Rivers, they were certainly not going to do it here at her house,' he thought.

"It's time for Sam Snyder to think about moving on," he decided, pushing an Oreo wrapper into his empty carton of milk.

20

"This Alaskan cruise Aunt Jean found for us is perfect!!" Liffey squealed from the dining room table.

She spread out a huge ship and shore travel brochure which included a map of Alaska and gestured at Sinead to come over and have a look.

Sinead looked doubtful as Liffey pointed out the ports of call on the ship's itinerary with a long kitchen knife.

"Not only does the cruise ship stop *here* at Anchorage, where Aunt Jean has discovered that there is a small school feis in May, but we can also go panning for gold *here* in the Yukon and take a small plane up *here* to Barrow to look for polar bears."

"And it will be midnight sun time in Alaska so we'll have daylight all the time. We'll never have to sleep!"

"Liffey, this is ridiculous. I can't afford that kind of trip. My dad would have a heart attack if I ever got up the nerve to even ask him about such a thing."

"And suppose we actually had the money? My parents would remind me that I am not long after having had my head cut open and that the doctors must have removed the common sense part of my brain by mistake."

"Sinead, in case you haven't noticed by now, money does not seem to be a problem around this place. Aunt Jean told me on the way to South Africa that we actually have an almost unlimited amount of it despite how my father acts all crazy whenever we spend it. She also said he has some kind of huge trust fund set up just to give money away to charities."

"Besides, your head is fine now and before you go back to Ireland, we need to do a feis together. I am sure that daddy would agree that you deserve a reward for all your bravery and your inspirational, positive attitude!"

Sinead grinned. She knew it was useless to take on Liffey Rivers when she had already made her mind up about something.

***

Peter Aleckson watched his favorite terrorist movie, *The Day of the Jackal,* on his iPad while he sat hidden in the bushes across the street from the Rivers' estate. He had always been fascinated by jackals. They were opportunistic carnivores that hunted alone. Like he did.

It was hard to believe how easy it had been for him to pull off an identity theft and be hired on as an employee of the prestigious Rivers Law Office's team of investigators.

'So much for thorough background checks,' he thought.

After being almost bored to death being trained by Sam Snyder's pathetic Kindergarten-level surveillance advice, he was equally bored now facing eight hours of purposeless observation time.

The ancient devices Sam had been using to keep track of the Rivers family were in the trunk of the leased black Mazda the Rivers firm had assigned to him. He had replaced Sam's toys with sophisticated spying equipment he had recently stolen from a careless CIA warehouse in Chicago.

It was not necessary for him to be vigilant watching the house or the grounds since he was the Rivers' worst nightmare—even though he was under strict orders not to do anything but keep his employer up to date with the Rivers family's day-to-day activities.

***

Maeve Rivers thought it was an excellent idea to take a cruise to Alaska and insisted that her husband lighten up a bit. "It would be wonderful to have an adventure together, Robert. It's been over four months since Sinead's surgery and Liffey has already finished her school assignments for this semester."

"I wish you would consider joining us, but I know better," Maeve said in her 'good sport' voice.

***

When Robert Rivers announced at dinner that he had agreed to their Alaskan cruise in early May, Liffey could barely finish her fried chicken. She excused herself from the table and ran down the hall into the library where she placed a call to her aunt.

"Aunt Jean, daddy caved in at dinner! We're going to Alaska!" Jean Rivers smiled victoriously and immediately went to work planning another trip of a lifetime.

***

Neil Patrick Roberts felt like he no longer belonged at the Holy Infant Home For Disabled Children.

He spent his days reading through 'get well' and 'thinking about you' cards, most of them from his friend Liffey Rivers, and doing excruciating physical therapy twice a day. Now that his legs had feeling in them, PT was like a bad dream.

99

Things had changed drastically since the huge black mamba had injected its poison into his withered legs. He felt like a white rat in a cage being studied by research scientists and doctors from all around the world.

After four months, they still turned up at the Home regularly and asked if they could "have a look-see" at him. Then they would jab at his legs to see where it hurt and he would inform them that it hurt everywhere they jabbed.

Thank God Sister Helen had put her foot down about removing him from the Home and placing him in a medical center in the UK.

"He is not a laboratory animal rat, doctors, and you may not treat him like one."

In spite of his PT pain and all the unsolicited medical attention, Neil was very excited about being able to walk for the first time in his life. There was only one hitch—he had nowhere to go.

***

Sinead debated with herself about whether or not she should tell her parents that she would be accompanying the Rivers on their cruise to Alaska. She knew it was wrong not to fill them in, but if she told them, their pride would rise up like a gale force wind. She could hear them now: "No! We McGowans do not take charity from anyone. Never did. Never will. The Rivers have already done far more for us than we are comfortable with."

She understood now why Liffey left out so many details when she told her father things. "Liffey is guilty of sins of omission, Sinead," Robert Rivers had told her once.

'Now I guess I will be too,' she thought uncomfortably.

21

The *Alaskan Sun* was looming up in the Vancouver Harbor like one of the snowcapped mountains in the distance. It was so big, it made Liffey feel like an insect.

"How can something that huge float?" Sinead asked wide-eyed.

Aunt Jean answered in her 'School of Life' teaching voice before anyone else had time to reply:

"Big Ships are assembled by boat builders, ladies."

Liffey looked away from her aunt at Sinead and tried not to giggle. Maeve looked down and pretended to cough.

Sheila Sullivan tried to salvage the moment and said, "So that's how it's done then."

"It's all about **buoyancy ladies**. These huge ocean liners are designed so that as they push down on the ocean, they displace a mass of water equal to their own mass."

Aunt Jean demonstrated this by pushing down and up with the palms of her hands.

"The pressure of the water pushing up on the bottom of the boat counters the downward force of the boat's gravity.

This is what keeps these huge ships floating on top of the water."

Sinead gave Liffey a surprised 'wonders never cease' look.

Liffey had to admit that her strange Aunt Jean was full of surprises. When she wasn't talking about make-up or practicing Irish dancing, was she reading science journals?

Sheila Sullivan had obtained medical passes for her two patients. This spared all of them from standing in a long line that went all the way back to the passenger terminal.

After they had presented their tickets and identification at the special needs check in desk, they were told to please step off to the right for a moment while the cruise director, who was personally greeting everyone, made a quick phone call.

Shortly thereafter, a handsome, white haired man with piercing brown eyes, wearing a white dress shirt with four gold stripes on each sleeve, introduced himself as Captain Dietz. He escorted them into the *Alaskan Sun's* atrium lobby with its eight circular balconies and domed glass roof. 'This ship is prettier than the *Titanic*,' Sinead thought as they entered a private elevator leading up to their suite.

"My crew has been ordered to attend to your every need, ladies," the Captain informed the speechless little group after he had supervised their suite inspection tour.

He gave a little bow from the waist and saluted them as he pressed the down button in the elevator and left them to marvel at their surroundings.

"Somebody pinch me, please!" Sinead said.

"He certainly is a looker," Aunt Jean predictably noted.

"I wonder how daddy managed to set all this up?" Liffey said, admiring the lavishly decorated, roomy quarters they were going to be floating around in for the next seven days.

There were four bedrooms jutting off from a large center sitting room that had two long couches covered with Chinese Modern blue, red and gold upholstery and six matching chairs. An entertainment center that had a large, flat screen television, computer terminal, and pool table adjoined the sitting room.

There was a separate dining room. On the table was a large vase containing two dozen mixed red, gold and blue roses matching the overall color scheme of the suite. A large picture window displayed the glimmering open waters waiting for them when they set off.

Sliding doors opened out from the entertainment center on to a private balcony with lounging chairs and recliners. There was a hot tub on another deck connecting with the balcony and up a small flight of stairs, yet another deck with a small swimming pool which could be filled if the weather permitted.

A Meade telescope inside a protective plastic cabinet was securely fastened to the lower balcony's railing just outside the sliding doors.

There were two bathrooms, each with two sinks and showers and one tub which, with the touch of a button, could be changed into a spa-like hot tub with water jets.

A full length, white terry cloth robe with the ship's logo and their own name embroidered on the front pocket, was hanging in each of their bedrooms.

Maeve watched Liffey taking in their new environment and said quietly, " Actually, Liffey, your father turned all the travel details over to me because I designed the family house and corporate offices for the owner of this cruise ship line when I was working as an architect in Chicago. He became a good friend over the years and knew all about my mysterious disappearance. When I called to ask him which cruise he recommended, he insisted on presenting us with this 'welcome home' gift. As a matter of fact, he and I are bartering a bit as well. He wants me to design a new headquarters for his company in Miami."

Liffey looked at her mother with new interest. She had never thought of her mother before as being a successful business person independent of her attorney father's success. This was a complete surprise.

She knew her mother had taken a leave of absence from her career as an architect when she was born, but she had no idea her mother had been designing mansions and corporate headquarters for people.

Doing a back-to-reality check, Sheila Sullivan insisted that Maeve and Sinead settle into one of the comfortable beds and take a short rest. "You two can get a little nap in and we'll all meet up out on the balcony when we hear the ship's whistle blowing," she ordered.

***

When Sinead had reluctantly resigned herself to a grown up 'time out' and closed the door of the room she would be sharing with Liffey, and everyone else was busy resting up after the long journey from Chicago to Vancouver, Liffey slipped out to the large, comfortable balcony to gather her thoughts.

She had been having strange dreams lately about polar bears and even today, right now in the middle of all this excitement, she had a sense of foreboding, like something very bad was just waiting to happen.

She knew that her father had grave reservations about this trip even though he had eventually agreed to it.

This meant he had detectives walking around the ship and that their owner's suite was not as private as they might think. After finding the tiny button camera on the plane to Amsterdam, Liffey now knew that surveillance was easily managed, no matter where you were.

She did not really mind all of her father's precautions, she was just sick and tired of always being only one small baby step ahead of the Skunk Man or Mr. McFleury or Donald Smith or whatever name he was using today.

'This has all got to come to an end soon,' she thought.

'I want to have a normal life again, even if it's boring.'

***

Mrs. Reginald W. Puce unpinned the iron gray wig which was styled into a sloppy bun on top of her head and placed it on the lowest shelf in Stateroom 304.

Mrs. Puce was traveling with three suitcases.

The smallest suitcase held two stylish gray wigs which were removed and placed on the shelf next to the drab bun wig along with hairspray and a large container of bobby pins

Tubes of ruby red and dark pink lipstick, two bottles of classic ivory Cover Girl foundation, round wire rim granny glasses, a pallet of eye shadow colors, makeup brushes to emphasize facial lines and premature wrinkles, pink vintage cat eye sunglasses, three strands of plastic bead necklaces with matching earrings, a full length body suit for shape alteration and a black metal fold-up walking stick were carefully arranged on a long vanity table.

The largest suitcase contained two pairs of sturdy walking shoes, three pantsuits in varying shades of blue, a warm dark blue jacket, two knitted hats with matching scarves and binoculars to keep Liffey Rivers in focus when they were on shore excursions.

The middle-sized suitcase contained a wardrobe for Plan B. 'There must always be a Plan B,' Mrs. Puce thought. 'Just in case Plan A fails.'

Identity theft was so easy. The real Mrs. Puce had no idea she had a double.

22

"Liffey," Sinead said tiptoeing through the suite out to the balcony, "do you think it might be okay if we left the cabin for a bit to have a look around the ship? I can't sleep. I'm too excited."

"Let's do it then!" Liffey agreed, happy that for a change it was not herself doing the scheming.

"My mother has not yet told us we are not allowed to leave the suite without her, so we had better go and do it now before she wakes up and says we can't."

"Besides, we need to find a practice place for the feis before we arrive in Anchorage and daddy probably has at least two detectives waiting to follow us around. We'll be fine."

Sinead laughed but Liffey could tell she looked uneasy.

"Anyway, I overheard my parents talking about how living like caged animals is no way to live."

***

Michael McGowan glanced over at his brother Eoin who was posted near the private elevator which led directly to the Rivers' suite. They wore the crew uniforms of the

Alaskan Sun. Michael had colored his hair prematurely gray and wore dark framed glasses.

Eoin had applied a dark foundation to give his fair Irish skin a Mediterranean look. He also wore eyeglasses with thick plastic lenses to hide his eyes and had grown a full beard which matched his dark brown hair.

Since they knew that their sister, Sinead, would not in a million years ever expect that her brothers were on board this ship with her, they felt fairly confident she would not recognize them.

When Robert Rivers had contacted them in Ireland about undertaking the undercover surveillance of their sister, it had seemed like a wonderful idea. Neither of them had traveled much and the idea of Alaska with its dramatic scenery and wildlife had greatly intrigued them.

There was also the fact that Attorney Rivers was paying the two McGowan brothers more money for two weeks work than they had made in the last six months working as Gardai detectives in Dublin. An added incentive was that they would also be coordinating their efforts with Interpol, something neither of them had ever imagined.

Attorney Rivers had instructed them not to tell anyone where they were going, even their parents, as Interpol insisted on total secrecy and was already second guessing Robert Rivers' decision to bring in the Anderson detectives from St. Louis and the two detectives from Ireland.

After they had been briefed by Interpol and they were officially totally responsible for their sister's safety, their carefree outlook had evaporated.

This was serious business.

Robert Rivers had said, "No matter how many elaborate precautions I take, gentlemen, there is a leak somewhere and Liffey's whereabouts are known. On several occasions, he or she has known where Liffey is even before I do. And now, there is also her mother to worry about. This has got to stop. People can't live this way."

When they had asked, "But why then take the risk?" Robert Rivers had told them that he was certain that this cruise was going to be the place where the man who was an on-going threat to his family would finally be brought to justice.

He had assured them Sinead would be safe since it would be their job to concentrate only on her. He explained he had hired five private detectives in addition to them and that Interpol had assigned an entire task force of agents to the *Alaskan Sun* to apprehend this terrorist.

***

Robert Rivers had secretly boarded the *Alaskan Sun* with Louise Anderson and her team of hand-picked detectives. He decided not to use his own law office investigators since so far, that route had proven to be very ineffective, and at this point, he suspected a mole. He sometimes thought his own staff made bad situations even worse.

His large stateroom on Deck 5 contained surveillance equipment interfacing with the mini cameras Louise had placed in strategic areas where she thought Liffey and Sinead were most likely to be—hallways, dining areas, the indoor pools, snack bars and the sprung stage floor in the Teen Scene Club.

Robert Rivers had been greatly appreciative when this international police enforcement agency had agreed to set up their own sting operation on the *Alaskan Sun*. The flow of conflict diamonds from Africa had been an ongoing, frustrating problem for them; and so far, while they had made much progress, they had not been able to completely dismantle the main operation headed by the elusive criminal who called himself the Raven.

Since Liffey Rivers and her mother were the only people known to Interpol who could positively identify the Raven by sight, they hoped to protect the Rivers ladies as well as rein in their South African diamond smuggler.

***

The elevator down indicator light went on and Michael McGowan switched on the ultra-mini video camera concealed in a pen in the right pocket of his uniform shirt. When he observed that Liffey and Sinead were the only passengers, he spoke into a tiny microphone hidden in his lapel and activated the 'two girls' alert: "The river is flowing."

"Get ready, Eoin, the girls are coming," he said tersely.

"Geez, this ship hasn't even left port yet," Eoin complained.

***

Liffey and Sinead were holding hands doing hop-one-two-threes along the ship's hallways when they rounded a corner too fast and body slammed into a family of four carrying oversized suitcases and four tennis rackets.

"Sorry!" both girls chorused.

"We're really awfully, terribly, so very, very sorry!" Sinead added.

Liffey thought she was seeing double. Directly in front her stood two of the cutest boys she had ever seen in her life and they both looked exactly the same. Dazzling smiles, liquid blue eyes, perfect chins, blond hair. They had to be identical twins.

Before Liffey could coordinate her brain with her mouth and say something intelligent, the family smiled politely, nodded, and moved past them on the other side of the hallway.

As the family of four moved out of sight, the twin boys looked back at Liffey and Sinead and flashed encouraging smiles.

Sinead said: "Liffey! There's one for each of us! *Please* tell me you know how to play tennis?"

"Not really," Liffey whimpered.

"I thought all rich people knew how to play tennis?"

"Daddy tried to show me a few times but I never liked it and I never thought it might actually matter so much someday."

"Well, you'll have to teach me the little you do know, Liffey, because we are going to find those twins and play tennis with them on this cruise!"

Before the girls could organize their next move, a loud whistle blasted a farewell salute to Vancouver Harbor.

"Time for roll call," Liffey said urgently. "Let's get back upstairs before we're missed!"

"I'll bet they have someone working on this cruise to teach people like us how to play tennis," Sinead said as they trotted back to the elevator.

"Good idea," Liffey said. "We'll find the tennis pro and then get to work immediately on our moves!"

Sinead began to laugh so hard at this remark that she could barely walk and could only manage to lean against the wall in the hallway and slide along it towards the elevator.

"Come on! Move it! We're going to miss the boat!" Liffey screeched, succumbing to Sinead's pointless hilarity and beginning to laugh uncontrollably herself.

"You don't want to see Nurse Sullivan's dark side, Sinead!"

"Or your mum's either, Liffey," Sinead managed to say, practically choking with laughter.

The elevator arrived in the suite and their hyena fits of screaming laughter ended abruptly when they were greeted by two adults with grim expressions and one adult with a broad smile on her face.

"Girls, good news!" Aunt Jean could hardly contain her enthusiasm.

"This ship has two colorists on staff at the salon. What do you say we all drastically change our hair color?"

Liffey seized this unexpected opportunity to escape. "That's a great idea, Aunt Jean. Let's go out on the balcony right now and after we are well out of the harbor, the three of us can discuss our options," she said, cupping her aunt's elbow and leading her out on to the balcony.

Maeve Rivers smiled to herself. Robert had warned her that Liffey was amazingly nimble at maneuvering her way around authority. This was the first example of what he must have meant when he had told her, "Liffey will never deliberately disobey you, Maeve, but if she thinks you will say 'no' if she asks you first, she will often do something before she is told not to do it, hoping that nobody will notice. But if they did notice, she will then apologize profusely afterwards for the misunderstanding."

***

"Can you even believe how immature those girls are?"

"I mean, really! Unbelievable!" Eoin shook his head and switched off the camera concealed in his wristwatch.

"No argument, brother, that surgeon in Wisconsin must have removed part of our sister's brain along with the tumor," said Michael.

"Interpol is going to have a tough time taking Liffey Rivers and her sidekick, Sinead McGowan, seriously if they watch this ridiculous video we just took of them on their first walk-about tour of the *Alaskan Sun*."

23

Sister Helen knew the time for her to talk with Neil about his family had finally come. He was mostly using a cane now instead of his walker, and the rehabilitation center in Cape Town talked of his being discharged in the near future.

Liffey Rivers had assured her that the Rivers family was in a position to step in and provide not only unlimited, unconditional love for Neil, but also access to any medical care he might need to continue his excellent progress.

When Sister Helen had told Liffey about the education trust fund set up for Neil's education, Liffey had said, "Sister, that money should be used for your other patients. Neil will have everything he will ever need with me and my family."

"We will make sure he visits with you in Johannesburg and you are welcome to come to the States yourself and bring other children along with you for long vacations with us. We'll pay for everything and no one will ever have to say good bye. I'll teach Neil how to Skype and you both can talk every day."

Sister Helen meditated and prayed for two days before she decided that now was the right time to tell Neil he had parents and a sister, after she checked first with Robert and Maeve Rivers. It was obvious that Liffey took herself seriously enough to offer Neil her family, but she needed to hear this from Liffey's parents. She would not risk breaking little Neil's heart if, for any reason, they were not interested.

If the Rivers were willing, she would gently tell Neil his missing family had surfaced. If Neil was at all hesitant about meeting up with them, she would delay things as long as she thought wise.

Tears came into Sister Helen's eyes as she recalled how for years, Neil would wheel himself into the waiting room at the Home each night at sunset and wait for his parents.

It seemed that now, they were finally coming for him after all.

***

Mrs. Reginald Puce checked in with Peter Aleckson, the newly hired investigator on staff at the Rivers Law Office.

He left his office and went out into the hallway to take the call.

"I can confirm that Liffey Rivers and her mother and aunt are definitely on the *Alaskan Sun* but that's all I can tell you at this time. Attorney Rivers is using a detective agency from St. Louis for their protection and there is no other information here at the office. He is supposedly out of the country himself, but I do not have any details. I think Mr. Rivers suspects a mole."

"Very well then," Mrs. Puce said. "I will not call you again unless I want you to do something in-house. Get a message to me if you learn more, and have a nice day in the Windy City, Mr. Aleckson."

***

After the mandatory emergency muster drill, the *Alaskan Sun* cruise began heading towards the Inside Passage, on its way to Ketchikan.

Soon, the impressive skyline of Vancouver with its shore-hugging, Canada Palace that looked like a horizontal birthday cake topped with white chocolate Hershey's Kisses, blended into low-lying clouds and disappeared from sight.

There was a shiver in the air and even though everyone wore a hunter green 'Bon Voyage' fleece lined gift jacket from Robert Rivers, the farewell to Vancouver balcony celebration ended abruptly when Maeve Rivers decided she was hungry and freezing.

"It's time for us to find some warm food, girls," she said.

"I do hope they serve salads on this cruise," Aunt Jean worried, sliding the glass balcony doors shut behind them.

"Me too," Liffey chimed in. "Imagining a world without lettuce is just too much to bear."

Sinead snorted and placed a hand over her mouth, trying not to start convulsing with laughter again.

"Maybe we had better start eating salads too, Liffey, to get in shape for those exhausting tennis games we will soon be playing."

"You play tennis, Liffey?" Maeve asked. "Your father never told me that."

"I played all through high school," Maeve said. "We were actually State champions my senior year."

"I would love to play with you and Sinead, and of course you too, Sheila and Jean."

"I pass," Sheila replied. "I brought three books with me that I intend to read."

114

"I have given up sports for the 'dance,' Maeve," Aunt Jean declared pompously.

Maeve nodded understandingly and looked away.

Sinead was thrilled. "Liffey told me she is dying to learn how to improve her tennis technique, Mrs. Rivers."

"That's true, Mother," Liffey said, throwing Sinead a 'stop it right now' look, "but I was also hoping you might watch us do our hard shoe steps. It's been months since either of us has competed."

"According to daddy, you are an amazing Irish dancer," Liffey smiled.

"Your father is easily impressed," Maeve grinned.

"It's nice of him to talk so highly of my abilities when I am positive he has never seen me dance! We met years after I had turned in my ghillies."

"So. When you girls find a suitable floor space, we'll get right to work."

Aunt Jean sighed loudly as she removed the green fleece lined jacket and slipped into the chic blue suede jacket she had selected for tonight's early dinner seating.

"I am really sorry that there is not going to be an adult level competition at the Anchorage Feis, Aunt Jean. I know how disappointed you were in Johannesburg when there wasn't one there," Liffey said.

"Yes, Liffey. It is very true that I have had some major letdowns lately, but it's all part of living the life of an artist."

"My day in the sun will come."

"I am sure it will, Aunt Jean, and you have totally earned it."

***

Maeve Rivers was well aware that her husband had hired protection for this cruise as a precaution and was very glad that he had. Otherwise, they would have to take their meals in their suite and avoid all contact with the other passengers and most of the crew on the ship.

"That would be no way to take a vacation, Maeve," Robert Rivers had told her. "The shore excursions are the best thing about taking an Alaskan cruise."

"Louise Anderson will be on board with her detectives and she will not let anything happen to any of you."

Attorney Rivers did not mention that he too was going to be a passenger on the *Alaskan Sun*, along with Sinead's brothers and many of Interpol's conflict diamond task force investigators.

He did not want to worry his wife.

***

Mrs. Reginald Puce dressed down for dinner, selecting a black polyester, two piece pants suit and white plastic beads and earrings thinking, 'I do not want to attract attention.'

'I wish to dine alone tonight at my table for one with its lovely views of the ocean and the table the Rivers family has reserved for the early dinner seating.'

Placing the wig was tricky. It did not matter that it was obviously a wig, because many elderly women resorted to wearing a wig when hair dye no longer succeeded in hiding their own hair's lost luster.

What *did* matter was that this drab, gray wig not call attention to itself because then catty women might notice and there would be second looks followed by rude staring, and it would not be long until one of the cats began to suspect that Mrs. Reginald Puce might actually be a man wearing a woman's wig.

'If this should happen, I will have to disembark at our first port of call in Alaska tomorrow morning before Attorney Rivers' minions on board convince the local authorities in Ketchikan that I am a person of interest.'

***

When Robert Rivers received the phone call from Sister Helen in South Africa informing him that his daughter had discovered that the young boy who had saved her life in Johannesburg was her brother and did he wish to meet him, he was stunned and speechless.

She explained to him that at Liffey's insistence, she had conducted a DNA test on the two of them and, as Liffey had suspected, they were siblings.

Sister Helen described the very strange circumstances surrounding Neil's arrival at the Holy Infant Home for Disabled Children in Johannesburg. He had been found on the chapel altar in the convent quarters, all alone, sitting in a stroller next to a suitcase and an athletic bag containing five billion South African Rand. The Sisters had no idea where he, or the money, had come from.

Robert Rivers confirmed that his wife, Maeve, had been pregnant when she went missing and presumed dead for the past ten years. He related how his daughter had somehow managed to reunite their family in Ireland and that his wife still had amnesia about many periods of her life.

"I was very hesitant to ask Maeve about what had happened to our baby, Sister, because it was obvious when we were reunited that she had no memory concerning her pregnancy. I believed that she had miscarried."

When Robert Rivers expressed amazement that Liffey had not told him about this turn of events in South Africa, Sister Helen told him that she had asked Liffey not to say anything about Neil until she determined that the time was right.

"You have an extraordinary daughter, Attorney Rivers. I have never met anyone quite like her anywhere. She has the gifts of precognition and discernment at a very young age. Neil is a fortunate little boy. I have always prayed there was something wonderful waiting for him out there in this big wide world."

"Sister Helen, we need to make a plan," Robert Rivers said emphatically, struggling to maintain his composure.

"I completely agree, Robert."

***

Sometimes, Neil imagined he was Peter Pan. When he was younger, he thought that maybe he really *was* Peter Pan because many of the stories about Peter Pan seemed to fit his own circumstances.

It made sense.

He, like Peter, had been lost by his own birth parents too when he was a tiny baby.

While he knew that most of the Peter Pan legends did not exactly fit, he imagined that, like Peter, he too would be able to fly if he conjured up happy enough thoughts. Maybe he had friends and adventures waiting for him back in Never Land if he could just figure out how to get back there.

So, when Sister Helen told him his parents had found him and that they lived in the United States, he was thrilled.

Neil had dreamed that he had parents somewhere who would find him someday.

Those parents did not have to be the birth parents who had lost him. Any kind of parents would have suited him just fine, but until right now, no parents, birth or otherwise, had ever come for him.

And the fact that he had saved his own sister, just like Peter Pan would have saved Wendy, made him feel like he was on his way back to Never Land to meet up with his real life again.

He could hardly stop himself from crowing with joy.

What more could he have ever hoped for?

Certainly he would miss Sister Helen and many of the other children and Sisters terribly, but she had assured him they would all get together often.

Maybe he was going to be able to fly after all if he kept having such happy thoughts.

24

Louise Anderson watched the Rivers group from her stateroom entering and then exiting their suite elevator. When they moved out of her monitoring range and into Robert Rivers' view of their table in the main dining room, Louise put on thick glasses and applied garish purple lipstick. Prior to this cruise, she had purchased a purple velvet pantsuit, a gold metallic blazer and several country western clothing ensembles for formal undercover dining.

'I cannot look much tackier than this,' she thought approvingly, smoothing a few purple velvet creases out of her jacket top as she headed out her room to take up her surveillance position.

The McGowan brothers moved into position on the first floor of the dining room, dressed as wait staff in white coats and black slacks.

Three of Louise Anderson's detectives were seated at tables on the balcony level of the dining room which provided them panoramic views of the first floor. The other two Anderson detectives were placed at tables in the middle of the first floor dining room.

Robert Rivers had dinner delivered to his stateroom and watched both levels of the dining room using hidden surveillance cameras which displayed images on a forty-two inch monitor.

Interpol agents were occupied at their command center analyzing the entire passenger manifest with all the high tech crime fighting tools they had at their disposal.

All of the documentation the passengers had provided was carefully scrutinized. The fingerprints that Canadian immigration had turned over to them were run through worldwide data bases.

Robert Rivers had convinced Interpol to make this operation part of 'Infra-Red,' their International Fugitive Roundup and Arrest task force. They hoped that Robert Rivers' hunch that the Raven would be on this ship was correct. If they could apprehend him on the *Alaskan Sun*, there would be irreparable damage done to the flow of blood diamonds out of Africa.

***

The wait staff at Table 17 serving the group of five ladies in the Rivers' party had been ordered to perform with flawless professionalism.

"This party of five is to be treated like royalty," the head waiter, Fritz, had instructed them. "CEO orders."

Fritz was a bit concerned that Sean, one of four junior waiters on his team for this sailing had just joined the staff at Vancouver and thus was untested. He would keep a close eye on this new Irish waiter and his beard would have to be trimmed.

***

Liffey's carefree mood had abruptly disappeared and she was obviously now out of sorts when Maeve asked, "Aren't you hungry, Liffey? I've never seen you turn down a good appetizer. Here, try one of these," she said, holding up a tempting platter of roasted jumbo shrimp.

Liffey forced a smile and answered: "I'm saving my appetite for dessert, Mother. The menu says it's strawberry cheesecake."

Maeve didn't believe her but said nothing and continued studying her daughter while she nibbled on an Alaskan smoked salmon roll.

'How do I tell everyone that my back feels like it's being embroidered with sewing needles and my arms feel like they're being electrocuted?' Liffey flinched, trying not to writhe with pain. 'And *how* does he always find out where I am?'

She decided to try the 'put your thinking cap back on your head' trick her father had taught her long ago and began a thorough analysis of the problem at hand.

'He's somewhere here in this dining room. I'm sure of it. So I had better tell someone quickly before he makes a move.'

'I have a mother now. She'll know what to do.' Liffey began to scribble a note to Maeve on her napkin with one of the short pencils left on the table for checking off dessert choices.

She stopped writing, however, when she thought about what would probably happen if she did pass a warning note to her mother—they would all race back to their suite and probably not leave it again for the duration of the trip.

On the other hand, this man was after her mother too. She could identify him immediately while Liffey would have to rely upon the warning pins and needle sensations and looking directly into his reptilian eyes.

'But Sinead will be so disappointed if we don't at least *try* to track the twins down for a game of tennis.'

Liffey wished desperately that her father were here with them. She had told Sinead that she was sure he would have hired detectives to follow them around but so far she had not been able to detect any.

She removed her phone from her shoulder purse and said, "Please excuse me for leaving the table at dinner but I forgot to tell daddy that Max is not eating well and that he needs to give him puppy food until his appetite comes back."

"I hadn't noticed Mr. Dog was not eating enough lately, Liffey, but go ahead and call home if you think your father should adjust Max's diet."

"Thanks. I'm just going to go over there closer to the picture window for better reception," Liffey added, moving quickly away from the dinner table, keeping her eyes focused on a cluster of plants near the wall.

She was somewhat consoled when her father answered on the first ring and before Robert Rivers could get a word other than "hello" out of his mouth, Liffey said softly, "Daddy, he's here on the ship in the dining room! I know it. I have major pins and needles. I can't remember them ever hurting this much before. What should I do?"

Robert Rivers drew in a deep breath and said: "Liffey, first you must act like we are having a normal conversation right now. Laugh a little bit and shake your head like I just told you a funny story. Make sure you don't look as tense as you sound. I'm on your ship too and…"

"You're *what* too?" Liffey interrupted.

"I'm on this *Alaskan Sun* cruise too. I'm sitting up in my stateroom studying surveillance camera video feed of the dining room. I can see you now standing by the plants talking on your phone. Louise is on board also with five detectives as well as both of Sinead's brothers. Right now she's sitting next to the front door in a purple velvet pants suit."

"Louise?"

"And the McGowan brothers are here too?"

Before Liffey could go on, her father cut in: "You need to go back to your table and act like nothing is wrong. One of your waiters is a McGowan making sure there is no food poisoning going on so it's safe to eat."

"I don't want that man aware that you are on to him. We will flush him out, Liffey, and you and your mother will be fine."

"Now here's what we'll do. I know that you are planning on going to the *Grease* revue after dinner. So after you eat your dessert, leave the dining room together and go directly to the theater."

"I will alert Louise and her staff right now and you will be surrounded by her five detectives when you exit the dining room. So please try to relax and enjoy the show."

"An Interpol detective will seat you in one of the private boxes and remain outside, guarding the entrance, until the show is over. The box is VIP seating and is shielded from view so no one in the audience will be able to see you."

"After the show, you will be surrounded again and escorted to your private elevator. I'm afraid you will have to spend the rest of the night in your suite until I get the surveillance and protection staff coordinated with this turn of events."

"Daddy, did you say Interpol is also on the ship along with Louise, her five detectives *and* the McGowans?"

"Isn't this all a bit much?"

"Liffey, that man has written the word 'victim' on your forehead. He has got to be extremely impatient by this time with his repeated failures. It is more than probable that he plans to carry out some new plan by himself."

"Interpol has told me he enjoys working alone and you and I know that he always uses elaborate disguises. It's almost as if that man invented the phrase, 'deep cover.' "

Liffey gulped and allowed her eyes to scan the guests seated throughout the dining room.

He could be anyone—a waiter, a passenger, even a ship's officer. He could be sitting anywhere, watching her every move. His disguises were always unique and detail oriented.

"We will figure things out, Liffey. Interpol has so many spy gadgets that I feel like I'm an extra in a James Bond movie. I promise that I am going to make it possible for all of you to enjoy your cruise in spite of this glitch. Please don't tell anyone about your suspicion. All of you will be surrounded from now on everywhere you go. When you return to your bedroom, look under your pillow. There will be a two-way wireless microphone for you to report to every agent on board if you feel the need. Wear it when you leave your suite and you will never be alone."

✳✳✳

Liffey returned to the table and reported that she and her father had a pleasant conversation and that Max was fine. She tried to look natural and calm but could tell that Sinead was giving her a 'what's up?' look.

"After the show ladies, we'll plan tomorrow's agenda," Maeve said, shooting Liffey a suspicious glance.

"We'll be docked at Ketchikan just before first light tomorrow morning. It's not a big place but there's lots to do. We'll see what our shore excursion options are."

Liffey tried not to show how uncomfortable and anxious she felt but suspected she was not fooling anyone, except for maybe Aunt Jean who said, "Yes! Let's do our hair makeover first thing in the morning girls before we get off the boat to shop. I think I am going to try ash blond or possibly chestnut."

'He must be very close,' Liffey thought. 'I can feel his eyes watching me.'

***

Mrs. Puce was watching Liffey Rivers closely and thought she detected a slight change in the wig girl's demeanor after she had finished the telephone call.

She ate the last bite of her strawberry cheesecake and sipped an excellent cup of Raven's Brew Coffee which came from Ketchikan where the ship would be docking tomorrow morning.

'Tomorrow I will buy as many packages of these magic coffee beans as I can fit inside my suitcase.'

A few years ago, Mrs. Puce had tasted this gourmet coffee for the first time when she had selected it because of its name from the menu of a five star restaurant in Tunisia.

Unfortunately, shipping Raven's Brew Coffee to South Africa was out of the question. Mrs. Puce never had any deliveries of any kind sent to either of her two permanent residences--the house in Johannesburg or the hunting lodge called, 'The Lion's Lair,' located on a private game reserve where she was known as 'Mr. Josef Brun,' a middle aged man with a heavy Swiss accent.

Mrs. Puce was very much enjoying this delicious, soul-warming Raven's Brew coffee, and allowed herself to drift off into a dreamlike state thinking about the Lion's Lair retreat back in South Africa. 'When I am done here, I will return to my den and perhaps stay forever, although I will certainly miss being 'The Raven.' She smiled to herself thinking of how in some groups of Native Alaskans, their mythology described the Raven as being the creator of the entire world and the bringer of daylight.

'Silly myth,' she thought. 'Ravens are just scavengers that will pick every last morsel of meat off the bones of other animals' dead prey. They feast off the efforts of others. Just like I do when I gather up my diamonds.'

The Lion's Lair was located in an untouched wilderness of 20,000 acres with a river running through it. There was a ridge of moody blue mountains in the distance and such an abundance of wildlife that it was possible to sit on the veranda for hours and observe all of the Big Five: lions, leopards, cape buffalo, rhino and elephants. There were also giraffes, herds of antelope and an occasional dazzle of zebras.

The Lion's Lair was exempted from following the game hunting rules of the Department of Nature Conservation in South Africa because it was privately owned.

Josef's reserve had high steel fencing surrounding it and all of the wildlife on it belonged to him. In any season of the year, he was free to track and kill as many animals as suited his mood. At times, he hunted his reserve animals so relentlessly, he almost fainted from over exertion.

He enjoyed his blood sport so much, he was running out of space in his large house for the heads of his trophy animals.

Mrs. Puce drained the last ounce of Raven's Brew from her blue china cup and stood up slowly, pushing off from the arms of the dining room chair like a woman in her late seventies might do to maintain her balance.

It appeared that the entire Rivers group was headed out the door where there was already a queue of passengers waiting for the second dinner seating.

***

When the applause had ended, Sinead pulled Liffey aside before they left their box seats.

"Either I am completely mental now, which is totally possible, or have we been being followed ever since we left the dining room?"

"No, you're not mental, Sinead. I noticed them too. I told you my father would have detectives on this ship. He's afraid my friend the Skunk Man will be on board to have another go at my mother and me."

"I can't say for sure how many, but I am certain that there are lots of people on this ship looking out for all of us while they are also trying to take out that slime ball."

"I heard the police in Johannesburg calling him, 'The Raven.' He's supposed to be some kind of international terrorist who runs a huge conflict diamond operation in South Africa, and they said that they have been trying for years to take him into custody."

In the hallway outside of the theatre, Sinead did her best not to stare at the men and women sauntering along in the front, back, and on each side of them on their way to their elevator.

After they had safely returned to their suite, Sheila Sullivan thought it would be a good idea for everyone to go to bed early since it had been a long day.

Sinead looked stricken.

"Oh please not yet! It's not even dark!" she pleaded.

Sheila disagreed and said, "Sinead, it's not going to get dark much. Remember, we're headed into the land of the midnight sun."

"Actually, Sheila, I agree with you," Maeve interjected. "But I was hoping we could all discuss what we want to do tomorrow before we turned in."

Sheila agreed. "Okay, but remember, my job here is to make sure you and Miss McGowan don't exert yourselves too much."

Maeve nodded and looked directly at Liffey. "At the risk of sounding like your dear father, Liffey, I am afraid a very short discussion about Ketchikan is in order."

Liffey braced herself and tried not to panic. This was the first real trip she had taken with her mother since she had been three years old.

What if her mother was as boring as her father? After all, they *were* married to each other so that meant that they probably shared common interests forever ago when they had dated.

What if her mother's idea of having fun was looking at crumbling old buildings and piles of old rocks just like her father?

"As I've said before, Ketchikan is small but has a lot going for it and we'll have nine hours to explore the area. The town is built on the bottom side of a mountain and it stretches about ten miles along the coastline."

'So far, so good,' Liffey thought. 'Daddy would have gone into lots more detail.'

"There are several fishing excursions we could book when we get off the ship, but I am thinking none of us would want to do that, unless you like to fish, Sheila?"

"I think I'll pass on that one, Maeve," Sheila said.

"Liffey, do you like to fish?"

'Was she kidding?'

"No thanks, Mother. Fishing is even more boring than daddy's history lessons. I used to pretend to like it out on the lake with him when I was little, but I hated watching all the fish we caught die. And all those poor worms...."

"Sinead, how about you?"

"Actually, Mrs. Rivers, I was hoping you might be able to help us with our tennis game tomorrow," Sinead said, trying not to look at Liffey and erupt with laughter again.

Finally, it was decided that they would have an early room service breakfast, disembark and visit two museums: the Totem Heritage Center and the Alaskan Discovery Center.

After lunch, when they returned to the *Alaskan Sun*, Maeve would demonstrate forehand and backhand serves and anything else she could remember from her tennis playing days.

Aunt Jean wanted to shop.

Shelia Sullivan thought she would do a few local tours.

***

In Ketchikan, after Sinead, Liffey and Maeve had reboarded the ship, Maeve left them and headed to the cruise director's office to reserve a tennis court.

Liffey had a single minded purpose with her sudden interest in tennis. She wanted to impress the twins.

She hoped she would be able to tell which one of them was the nicest, or at least the smartest. She had had quite enough of all the stupid, annoying boys at her old middle school, also known as, Principal Godzilla's Penitentiary, in Wisconsin.

Liffey knew that identical twins were not necessarily identically smart or equally interesting, because after all, they did have separate brains.

If one of the twins turned out to be a dud, she would steer him towards Sinead who had made it very clear she did not care which one of them she ended up with.

When they reached the court, they saw two tennis rackets abandoned on a ledge and Sinead suggested they try to volley the ball while they waited for Maeve to return.

"When you play tennis and just volley the ball, it's like volleyball except the ball is not meant to touch the ground and bounce more than once, Liffey," Sinead instructed.

She hit a slow, underhand serve over the net to Liffey. "You know, it's kind of exciting having bodyguards, Liffey, it's like we're famous or something."

"Maybe," Liffey replied, effortlessly returning Sinead's serve.

Volleying was easier than she had thought it would be and in between returning the ball, Liffey found herself thinking about their visit to Ketchikan earlier in the day.

Ketchikan had been interesting even if it was touristy. Learning about the Southeastern Native Alaskan cultures had been an eye-opener for Liffey.

There had been totem poles almost everywhere they went. Even outside of the Totem Heritage Center there were new totem poles carved from red cedar wood. One of them smelled like the inside of her mother's cedar chest.

Until this morning, Liffey had not had any idea that there were so many tribes within each of the Native Alaskan cultures. It was impossible to remember most of them, but she did remember that the Tlingit culture was the most prominent one in the Ketchikan area.

"I feel so stupid, Sinead, until today, I actually thought all Native Alaskans were Eskimos," Liffey said, shaking her head with disgust, missing the ball for the first time.

"And I also thought that totem poles were worshiped, which they never were," Liffey said hitting the ball with an easy underhand serve.

"They're like an outside art gallery of sculptures with carved stories of their myths and tribal symbols just like the Irish have their family crests."

Liffey could feel the wheels spinning in her head and had already decided that when she got back to Wisconsin, she was going to carve a Rivers family totem pole to place at the entrance to their lake estate driveway. She knew she could count on Aunt Jean to help.

Sinead too had been fascinated by the totem poles in Ketchikan, but had become more fixated on the facts that eating the cooked eyes of salmon and sliced up moose noses were considered delicacies by many Native Alaskans.

"Liffey, how can anyone eat fish eyes and jellied moose noses and not gag to death?" Sinead asked, lobbing the ball high over the net.

Liffey managed to hit it back.

"Well, how can you eat black pudding in Ireland for breakfast, Sinead?"

Sinead missed the ball and served again.

Liffey hit it back. "If I recall, it's made from pork fat and pig's blood."

Sinead returned the ball.

"Fair enough. But what about 100% pure cow or pig guts American hot dogs?"

Liffey slammed the ball over the net and it bounced out of bounds.

"What about pig trotters, Sinead?"

"What about *what*?"

25

"**G**irls, I'm very sorry it's taken me so long to get back. Getting this tennis court was more time consuming than I had expected. There were three other families in line and one of them actually gave up their place for us when they heard me say I was going to teach you two how to play. And there were also two very handsome young men in line—identical twins in fact, who offered their assistance and I told them we would be delighted."

Liffey felt her heart thumping so hard in her chest she was afraid it might burst out.

"And when would this be, Mother?"

"Soon. A bit later this afternoon at 4:30. They were going to have a family foursome but the boys asked their parents if they could help both of you instead and their parents said it was fine with them."

Liffey tried not to shriek like a madwoman when she said: "But Mother, Sinead and I don't know *how* to play tennis!" Her dream of impressing the twins with her skillful backhand was turning into a disaster.

"I explained all that, Liffey. They said they'd be happy to teach you and I just assumed you might prefer…"

"Of course we'd prefer the twins, Mrs. Rivers. Nothing against you of course but they are very fit and…"

Liffey cut in. "Sinead! Enough already!"

"Oh, so you already know who they are then?" Maeve asked with twinkling eyes.

"Yes, Mother, we know who they are. We almost knocked them to the ground yesterday while they were walking down a hallway to their stateroom. I'm sure they'll recognize us immediately and then run for their lives."

"Actually, I think they might know who both of you are already, Liffey. I mentioned that my daughter and her guest from Ireland wanted to learn how to play tennis and that I hoped I could remember my long ago moves and one of the twins smiled and said, "The one from Ireland likes to apologize, right?"

Sinead cringed.

"Okay, then. Time to work, girls." Maeve was suddenly all business.

"Another group has the court in forty-five minutes. I can teach you the basics pretty quickly. By 4:30 both of you will be pros."

***

Mrs. Puce had used her short excursion to Ketchikan to purchase twenty-five packages of Raven's Brew coffee beans to take back with her to South Africa. The totem poles interested her and she thought about commissioning a few to be carved for her Lion's Lair reserve. But then they might draw unwanted attention. She imagined a tall pole with a carved lion's head followed by an elephant and then a rhino… Maybe she would carve them herself and place the poles just off the veranda where they would not be visible to the outside world.

It amused her to see so many detectives surrounding Maeve and Liffey Rivers and their group wherever they went. It was very apparent that Robert Rivers' wannabe detectives from St. Louis thought they needed to protect his little family 24/7 but this had been expected and she was prepared to wait until the very end of this relaxing cruise, if it came to that, to make her move.

In fact, the more she thought about it, it might be best to wait for the shore excursion to Barrow. She would stick to her original plan unless an opportunity presented itself on board beforehand. The media often had reports of mysterious disappearances of passengers from cruise ships.

Mrs. Puce was enjoying this cruise so far. The chilly, wet weather reminded her of her past life in Seattle where she had been Donald Smith taking care of his drugged, helpless 'sister,' Mary, his most successful diamond smuggler to date, even with her chronic amnesia.

The elderly Mrs. Puce was content to walk around the viewing deck or sit in a comfortable lounge chair near the railing, wrapped up in a warm blanket the crew provided along with a cup of hot chocolate. The waterfalls trickling down the mountains in the inner passage reminded her of runny icing on a birthday cake with too many candles.

So far, the wildlife she spotted on the shores of this inner passage did not interest her much. An occasional eagle and a few deer, although the naturalist on board said they might expect to see whales, bears, moose, seals and perhaps dolphins later on during the trip.

Mrs. Puce saw more wildlife in ten minutes sitting outside on the veranda of her Lion's Lair than she had on this entire trip so far.

***

"We've got exactly fifteen minutes to look amazing, Liffey. Do you think it can be done?"

"No, Sinead. I don't think I could look amazing if I had fifteen days to work at it. But you have more to work with than I do so let's concentrate on you."

"Liffey, shut up! You know that you're absolutely gorgeous," Sinead said irritably.

Liffey thought back to the painful days at her middle school in Wisconsin and the cruel remarks other girls made about the way she wore her hair and ridiculed her because she never wore makeup to school. The girls even made fun of the clothes she wore.

Aunt Jean had tried to be a mother. But Aunt Jean's idea of suitable school attire was *haute couture* with a twist— clothes that looked like they belonged on Lady Gaga, not on a middle school student in Wisconsin.

She had endured her primary school years with the same group of mean girls. Once, in second grade, she had mistakenly worn a two-piece plaid pajama set to school that her Aunt Jean had given her.

Liffey had been sure that it was a matching slacks and top ensemble. Her father had even noticed it and told her how nice she looked that day when she ran out of the house to catch the school bus.

When she arrived in her home room, the entire class had made fun of her and called her "Pajama Girl" until the teacher firmly put a stop to it.

Normally, the harassment had not bothered Liffey too much because she considered the source: girls who were even more pathetic and stupid than the idiot boys in her school.

However, with this tennis lesson just minutes away, her confidence was at an all time low.

Liffey Rivers might know how to take out international terrorists but she had no idea how to act 'cool' with her peers.

Until she had met Sinead in Ireland at the Beltra Feis, she had no close friends.

She decided now that she wanted to help Sinead with the twins and forget about even trying to make herself look like someone she was not. What was the point? If one of the twins was not going to like her for herself, then that was his problem.

When Maeve Rivers finally returned to the suite after disappearing on the way back from the tennis court, she reported: "Girls, you only have ten more minutes until your tennis lesson and you can't play tennis properly wearing jeans and sweatshirts. Since we did not pack for tennis and both of you have to be able to move around on the court comfortably...I've done some shopping!"

Maeve handed Liffey and Sinead one bag each.

"I found a bargain barrel outside of a shop—a 'two for one' sale already marked down 50%, so I couldn't resist. The matching jackets came with the tennis dresses. I am thinking that this boat must have been sailing in a warmer climate before its Alaskan cruise season began."

"Hot pink for you, Sinead and lilac purple for you, Liffey. I think the tennis dress sizes should be about right and now you can both learn to play and have the mobility you need to move quickly and hit that ball."

"Both of you already have suitable shoes."

"There's no need to worry about hair or makeup girls," Maeve commented, watching Sinead experimenting with her own hair which had almost fully grown back in again since her surgery.

"Playing tennis is about getting regular, good exercise and mastering a fun sport."

Liffey ran over to Maeve and hugged her. She felt like crying for joy. It was so wonderful having a mother again.

***

The Interpol agents on board the *Alaskan Sun* were very frustrated. They had used all the standard background check systems at their disposal and so far had not come up with any likely suspects.

The Raven was as elusive as ever.

One last identity detection screen would be run—a more sophisticated, biometric fingerprinting analysis system developed in Switzerland that could reveal the slightest aberration on someone's fingertips.

If someone on this ship had deliberately altered their fingertips, it was almost a given that one or more of the patterns on their fingertips would reveal this.

Prior to boarding, all passengers had been required to have all ten of their fingertips printed. Interpol had hopes that the Switzerland system would flush out the Raven if he was on the *Alaskan Sun*.

If the state-of-the-art fingerprinting technology did not turn up one or more persons of interest, then the Interpol agents would disembark at the next port and end their participation in this manhunt. According to headquarters, it would take approximately three days to get the Switzerland analysis.

***

Louise Anderson was as frustrated as Interpol. Neither she nor her detectives had yet been able to turn up a likely suspect. Her entire team followed Liffey and Maeve Rivers and the rest of the group whenever any of them left their suite. One of her detectives was still ashore shadowing Jean Rivers who was apparently on a buying spree at the shops in Ketchikan.

Robert Rivers went over the surveillance tape he had from last night when Liffey was talking with him on the phone and had told him she was experiencing severe warning pins and needles.

This would indicate that the Raven/Skunk Man/feis judge Donald McFleury/Donald Smith and whoever he was disguised as now on this ship, had been very close to Liffey in the dining room.

He was missing something on this tape.

He knew it.

He reviewed the surveillance tape for the fourth time and concentrated on an elderly woman sitting by herself at a window table approximately twenty-five feet from Liffey. She was leisurely eating dessert and sipping coffee or tea. She was also watching his daughter while she talked on the phone. Was this suspicious behavior by a man disguised as an old woman or was she merely a lonely old woman?

Directly across from this woman was a man sitting in a wheelchair facing Liffey at his dining table and he too was looking at Liffey. This man could easily be the Raven.

In back of the suspicious elderly woman's table was a very masculine looking lady wearing a tweed suit. She had leathery, overly tanned skin and her dyed blond hair had light brown highlights. She too had a sight line which included Liffey and stared first at Liffey but also at the dining table where Maeve was sitting with her group.

Robert Rivers' intuition told him that one of these passengers was their target. At any rate, his hunch had to be checked out.

He flagged and sent the three suspicious images to Interpol, Louise and the McGowan brothers.

26

As Liffey and Sinead approached the tennis court, with Maeve following from a comfortable distance, Liffey hoped that she would fall and twist her ankle and have to be immediately taken to the ship's infirmary or better yet, transferred to shore by Ketchikan medics to a local hospital where she would be told she had to stay completely off her feet for at least six months. Only this scenario would prevent her from making a total fool out of herself again in front of the twins.

When Sinead saw them on the court slamming the tennis ball back and forth, she groaned. "Liffey, just look at them! How are we supposed to not look like total eejits?"

Before Liffey could ask her exactly what total 'eejits' were, the boys noticed them approaching and smiled and waved.

Liffey was afraid that she might faint and Sinead was no help when she said: "Liffey, I can't do this 'one on one' tennis lesson thing. I've never even been on a mixed group date. I go to an all-girls school where a boy sighting causes collective hysteria."

Liffey was surprised that she suddenly felt serene and detached. "Well, Sinead, I used to go to a school that had lots of boys and I am thinking that the word 'eejits' you just used would probably describe every last one of them."

Liffey flashed back to the lunchroom at her middle school to the time she had successfully fought off the stupid boy who had tried to steal her dessert brownie from her lunch tray.

"These twins are probably eejits too."

"They might be eejits but they are definitely classy ones, Liffey. Look, they're coming over to collect us!"

The two identical golden boys sauntered over to Liffey and Sinead and introduced themselves.

"I'm John," said one of them.

"I'm Luke," said the other one.

"Liffey Rivers," said a disembodied voice that sounded remarkably self-assured and pleasant. She extended a hand to each of the twins with a firm handshake.

Sinead stared at the twins speechless, with a deer in the headlights look on her face, until Liffey jabbed her in the side.

"Oh! I'm sorry!" she said. "I'm Sinead. Actually I'm Sinead McGowan. I'm from the Ursuline Convent School in Sligo."

"Are you going to become a nun?" one of the twins asked.

"She means she goes to the Ursuline College," Liffey interrupted.

"You're already in college?" the other twin asked.

"No. No. I'm sorry!" Sinead cried out.

"We're both going to be freshman in high school this fall," Liffey tried to explain.

"I'll be in third year," Sinead said.

"You'll only be in third grade?" a twin asked.

"No! I'm sorry! I meant I'm going to be doing my Junior Cert."

"Your what?" asked the other twin.

"I'm sorry. It's meant to be a big exam to prepare us for the bigger Leaving Certification Exam in 5th year unless we do a transition year, then the exam would be in 6th year."

"But for me," Sinead went on like a machine gun emptying a volley of bullets, "it could actually be 7th year because my mum might not let me do the 3rd year Junior Certification Exam this year because of my tumor."

Both twins looked alarmed.

"Oh, I'm so sorry, I should have said my brain tumor!"

Liffey tried not to freak out and attempted to salvage the situation.

"She means her ex-tumor. It's all been taken care of. She's fine. Now, let's play tennis, shall we? I promise Sinead won't flatline," Liffey said, placing her hand firmly under Sinead's elbow and leading her on to the tennis court.

The twins shrugged and nodded pleasantly like it had all been an ordinary conversation.

One twin took Liffey by the hand and walked her over to the other side of the court.

The other twin stayed at Sinead's side and gently moved her arm back and forth demonstrating the correct way to hit a tennis ball.

Liffey's twin turned out to be John and as they looked into each other's eyes, Liffey completely forgot that they were there for a tennis lesson.

"Know any good Knock-Knock jokes?" he asked, trying to break the ice.

Liffey smiled and answered: "Sure."

"Knock, Knock."

"Who's there?" John asked.

"Tennis."

"Tennis who?"

"Tennis-see!"

"You do know, don't you, that is one of the worst Knock Knock jokes I've ever heard," said John, fighting to keep the broad grin that was beginning to spread entirely over his face in check.

Liffey replied, "I can do worse."

***

Aunt Jean was running as fast as she was able to under the circumstances.

Not only was she completely worn out from trying on fur coats most of the day in the Ketchikan furrier shops, she was also struggling now under the weight of so many bags and packages.

"Noooooo!" she screamed when she heard a ship's whistle blasting its farewell to Ketchikan Harbor.

The *Alaskan Sun* was not yet in sight and she feared it was going to leave without her. Just when she thought it was hopeless and that she would be left behind, a thirty-something man came up from behind her and offered to help her carry her shopping spoils.

The two of them walked quickly, side by side, when she suddenly shrieked again: "Look! There are three ships in port now. How will we ever be able to tell them apart?"

'Louise wasn't kidding when she told me this lady was not playing with a full deck,' the helpful man thought.

"Our ship will say *Alaskan Sun* on its side in great big letters," the helpful man said. "The whistle is coming from another ship already leaving the harbor. Look, and you can see that it's beginning to move out."

Jean Rivers did not seem to think it was odd that the man accompanying her back to her ship knew which of the three ships was hers without her telling him.

From a nearby deck chair, unseen by Liffey and Sinead, Maeve Rivers studied the interaction between Liffey and one twin and Sinead and the other twin and her mother's alarm system went off.

'Those boys are *way* more sophisticated than either of these girls,' she thought worriedly.

It was obvious to her that Liffey was in way over her head already. She was absolutely radiant. Smiles beamed from her soft, lovely face like flood lights and Sinead was shining like the sun at high noon.

The twins, on the other hand, were apparently enjoying the girls' company but hardly falling head over heels in puppy love.

In fact, Maeve thought that they looked mildly amused and even somewhat detached, like they were used to adoring girls at their feet.

Maeve so wished that she had been with Liffey for the past ten years. 'I could have prepared her for this kind of encounter.'

'But I suppose a mother can never adequately prepare her daughter for her first overwhelming crush.'

'It's probably already too late. I will have to prepare myself for damage control later,' she thought sadly.

***

"Well that went well, brother," said Michael McGowan. "We have really got to have a word with our sister. She's a complete mess around boys."

"What do you expect? She hasn't gone to school with any male humans for years now," Eoin replied.

"And from what I just watched, those two lads appear to be deadly smooth."

27

"**I** can't *believe* that they really want to meet up with us tonight at the Teen Scene, Liffey!"

"Actually, Sinead, they said they would *probably* see us again soon at the club. Not that they were going to *meet* us at the club tonight. If we even go."

Liffey would not allow herself to shriek with joy. She had rarely been this elated. It was almost comparable to being reunited with her mother--not *that* good, but close. It seemed that the most awesome boy she had ever met so far in her life might actually be interested in her!

Maeve Rivers materialized and asked how the tennis lesson had gone.

Both girls smiled at each other and sighed.

✳✳✳

"Okay ladies. This sprung stage is perfect. We will begin with some warm ups before we start working on your treble jigs and hornpipes."

"Liffey, you will start with thirty jumping jacks. Sinead, you will only do ten. We are not going to push anything aerobic on you without a doctor's go-ahead."

145

Liffey could hardly believe that she not only had her mother back now but she also had her very own Irish dance teacher as well. After the feis in Anchorage, there would be many summer feiseanna and her mother had promised that they could go to several of them. It was hard to imagine going to a feis with your mother.

As for Aunt Jean's career as an adult Irish dancer, now that Maeve Rivers had returned and the Rivers' dining room had undergone removal of 'feng shui' influences, with all of the original furniture back in place, her aunt had joined an Irish dance school which catered to adults. Aunt Jean wanted to go to summer feiseanna where there would be adult competitions and had promised that she would take Liffey to any feis that her mother did not want to travel to.

Liffey had noticed that her aunt's post traumatic bling disorder did not seem to be a problem any longer and felt comfortable now about going to another feis with her. At least Aunt Jean deserved another try.

Sheila Sullivan slipped quietly into the room which would become an under sixteen disco at 8:00 p.m. with live entertainment. She could see that Sinead appeared to be in some kind of manic state.

"Sinead, are you experiencing anything unusual?" she asked. This question sent Sinead into another paroxysm of laughter like crashing into the twins yesterday had brought on.

Sheila Sullivan said, "And this is funny? I need to know how you are feeling, Sinead, before you start exerting yourself. That's why I'm here."

Liffey said, "Sinead's okay, Sheila. She's still just a bit loopy after working so hard at our tennis lesson."

"Well I'm going to watch to make sure if you don't mind."

"That's fine with me, Miss Sullivan," Sinead said, trying to catch her breath. "I'm sorry to keep laughing like this...."

***

Aunt Jean began organizing her shopping bargains from Ketchikan. It was refreshing to get back to the basics here in Alaska.

Mother Nature.

No more glitter and sparkle.

Wildlife.

Liffey would *adore* the bald eagle, mountain goat, musk ox, and dancing polar bear cubs T-shirts. The owl pajamas were inspirational.

Sinead would be *thrilled* with the three leaping salmon, the bear in the creek holding a salmon in its mouth and the caribou and wolf T-shirts. The matching owl pajamas were a hoot.

For Maeve, there was a moose sweat shirt because she was always cold on deck, along with walrus, bear cubs and sea lion T-shirts.

For Sheila Sullivan there was a whale T-shirt and a sky-blue sweatshirt with three soaring eagles and a plaid shirt.

'Call me selfish if you must, but I am keeping the dolphin sweatshirt for myself,' she thought, placing the final extra large grizzly bear sweatshirt back into its bag for Robert Rivers when they returned to Wisconsin.

She looked forward to receiving her other purchases which were being shipped home. There was a wooden couch with carved grizzly bears and other Alaskan animals she had purchased in a totem pole shop, and a full length fur coat she had ordered even though she did not believe anyone should own a real fur coat. She was not sure what kind of animal fur the coat was made from, but the furrier assured her that the poor animal had already been dead when its fur was removed for her coat and that made her feel much better.

***

The early dinner seating on the second day of the *Alaskan Sun's* voyage through the Inner Passage was uneventful. The ship would reach Icy Strait Point the next morning at 9:00 a.m. and there would be an eight hour layover for shore excursions.

Liffey did not feel any eyes boring into her brain this evening and there was a very nice string quartet playing Vivaldi. There were no pins and needles warning her to keep a close watch on her surroundings tonight.

The twins had said that they preferred eating casually in the buffet dining room and Liffey planned to announce to her group after this formal dinner that she and Sinead would prefer a less structured environment as well.

***

Robert Rivers looked closely at every table in the dining room with his hidden cameras and did not see any of the suspicious people he had singled out at last night's dinner.

***

Louise distributed the images Robert Rivers had forwarded to her from last night's dinner but none of her detectives had located any of the suspects in the dining room during the second night of formal dining on the *Alaskan Sun.*

***

Mrs. Reginald Puce had opened her Plan B suitcase prior to coming to dinner tonight and was now dressed as a scholarly-looking man wearing a three piece, wrinkled, dark blue suit. Dr. Lionel Nicholson, who was a professor of English Literature at a small Midwestern college, had sideburns and his hair was graying around the edges. He had a very pronounced overbite created by the mouth piece

148

insert he had wedged tightly against his upper teeth. Dr. Nicholson brought a thick history book along as his dinner companion.

He was seated at the opposite end of the dining room from the Rivers' table and was not particularly interested in what its occupants were doing at the moment. Yesterday, the professor had detected multiple surveillance cameras throughout the dining room and had counted at least five detectives surrounding the Rivers group whenever they left their owner's suite.

He had also noted the two men dressed as ship's officers who were always in the vicinity of Liffey and her girlfriend. He was not yet sure who these pretend officers were working for but he intended to find out. Perhaps they were with Interpol. Perhaps not. So far he had not seen any sign of Interpol's being involved here on the *Alaskan Sun* but it would not surprise him if they too were on board doing what they did best—analyzing data.

His primitive survival instinct told him that there was a big problem looming ahead for Mrs. Reginald Puce. He was not quite sure yet what it was but he knew he would soon need a stolen passenger swipe card to get off this boat before whatever disaster was waiting for him struck. His gut told him that Mrs. Reginald Puce was not going to be safe for much longer even though he had taken every precaution. He had even had his fingerprints surgically altered prior to this cruise. The plastic surgeon had used skin grafts from his toes.

It was time to play 'bribe the crew' and take the upper hand here in this amateur detective charade.

Give someone two years wages for a few small favors and they will do almost anything for you.

Along with a bogus or stolen passenger swipe card, Dr. Nicholson was also in need of a passengers' manifest, an unoccupied stateroom where he could immediately relocate until the next port of call and a list of shore excursions with the names of all the passengers who had signed up for each one of them.

Dr. Nicholson's internal danger alarm sounded before he had finished his second cup of Raven's Brew coffee.

He stood up abruptly, dabbed his face with a yellow linen napkin and walked swiftly out of the dining room to make a few emergency phone calls. He trusted his survival instinct completely. That was why, after all these years, he was still alive.

***

"Liffey, we cannot wear these ridiculous animal kingdom T-shirts tonight!" Sinead argued quietly. "Your aunt acts like she is expecting us to! I'm not going to go to the disco if I have to show up dressed like an eight-year-old."

"Let me handle it, Sinead."

"Aunt Jean, would you mind terribly if tonight Sinead and I wore the spaghetti strap dresses with the matching scrunch blazers you helped us find at the mall instead of one of the great T-shirts you got for us today?"

Sinead held her breath as she watched Aunt Jean's eyes flitting around the room like a moth looking for a place to land.

"Of course I don't mind, girls! Why in the world would I? The nature-themed attire should obviously be worn *only* for casual outings."

Maeve smiled nervously. She knew that Liffey had never been to any kind of an all-teen gathering place before. Since both girls would be shadowed by the detectives Robert Rivers had employed for this cruise, there was nothing to worry about. Except everything.

28

The Teen Scene club appeared to be almost full. It was very dark inside and a panel of pulsing strobe lights was splattering the faces of the crowd with a multitude of colors, making it difficult to recognize anyone from where Liffey and Sinead were standing.

"Liffey, do you think we're overdressed?" Sinead asked anxiously.

"No," Liffey replied. "I think we both look great!"

"Anyway, you're supposed to be the expert, Sinead. You've already been to three discos in Sligo," Liffey said, wondering why regular dances in Ireland were called discos.

"You cannot compare those disgusting discos in Sligo with this place, Liffey. In Sligo, the discos are held in awful places with slimy concrete walls dripping with condensation and disgusting loos full of underage idiots getting sick from the drink they managed to sneak inside."

Liffey shuddered. She had imagined that a teen disco in Ireland would be fun and romantic, not depressing and disgusting.

"I guess we should go in then," Sinead said after a long pause.

"I guess so," Liffey said. "We're both fourteen now. I suppose it's time to pretend we know how to have fun."

Both girls continued staring into the darkness. Neither one of them moved until after five minutes, when one of the twins suddenly appeared at the door and gestured for them to follow: "Come with me girls. We have a table."

Sinead poked Liffey so hard in the side it hurt and said, "I *told* you they were planning to meet up with us, Liffey!"

"Which twin are we following?" Liffey asked, making her way past the DJ playing throbbing music and pushing through the crowd gyrating on the sprung stage floor they had practiced their Irish dance steps on a few hours ago.

"Mine or yours?"

Liffey wished she had not come. She had never danced before except for Irish dancing and was not at all sure how she could avoid looking totally stupid if her twin wanted to dance.

***

Louise and three of her detectives were busily occupied looking for Puce video footage from the *Alaskan Sun's* elaborate security system's cameras.

So far, they had found only two images: one of Puce boarding the *Alaskan Sun* in Vancouver and another of her re-boarding in Ketchikan.

Mrs. Puce had obviously been keeping a low profile.

The other two Anderson detectives were standing outside the teen club watching who went in and came out.

The McGowan brothers were patrolling the deck and hallways feeding into the club area.

So far, their undercover surveillance work had been dull and routine.

They were thinking maybe Robert Rivers might have guessed wrong about the Raven being on this cruise.

It was already after 10:00 p.m. and Liffey knew that her 11:00 p.m. curfew would arrive long before she wanted this evening to end. So far, it had all been magic.

She discovered she was actually a good dancer, and she could not remember anymore what she had been afraid of.

John was funny and very attentive. She felt like she was the only girl in the room and from the looks of it, Sinead seemed to be having an incredible time too.

When it was 10:50, Liffey stood up from the table and announced that they had to go and was thrilled to see that John looked disappointed.

He stood up, leaned across the table and before Liffey knew what was happening, she felt his lips brushing against hers.

A kiss!

Was this her first kiss?

She tried not to look too shocked and gave him what she hoped was an encouraging smile.

"Good night, then. I had a great time," John said.

Sinead had a deer-in-the-headlights look on her face again, so Liffey thought that the same thing must have happened to her too.

She prayed Sinead would not start shrieking until they were well away from the club.

***

Maeve Rivers pretended to be asleep in her bedroom when she heard Liffey and Sinead racing into the living room from the elevator. From the way they sounded, things had gone well for both of them.

29

*A*t 10:00 a.m., a ripple of excitement went through the Interpol command center. They had received notice of a suspicious fingerprint result from the biometrics lab in Switzerland, even though they had not expected any results for at least another twenty-four hours.

It was a very subtle anomaly, but the opinion of the lab was that a passenger calling herself, 'Mrs. Reginald Puce,' who boarded the ship at Vancouver, had surgically altered her fingerprints.

The Swiss lab had red-flagged the Puce passenger for interrogation and further background data checks.

When Robert Rivers learned of the lab's finding, he was certain about his hunch that the old woman watching Liffey talking on the phone on his surveillance tape had been the Skunk Man in disguise. All they needed to do now was to quickly move in and apprehend him, and his family's long ordeal would finally be over.

An Interpol agent wearing a maintenance uniform was immediately stationed outside of the Puce stateroom with a toolbox and as soon as the proper paperwork was in order, 'Mrs. Puce' would be formally detained for questioning.

Shortly thereafter, a 'person of interest' arrest would be made.

***

Professor Lionel Nicholson looked down at Icy Strait Point from the 10:05 a.m. daily flight to Anchorage. Earlier, after a quick shopping spree where he had purchased a warm parka, insulated gloves, boots and two sets of thermal underwear, he had taken a cab to the airport where he presented the 'Hoonah-to-Juneau-to-Anchorage' ticket he had purchased online and bade the *Alaskan Sun* farewell as his plane took off and banked west.

From Anchorage he would travel to Barrow, Alaska, where he would wait for Liffey Rivers and her mother.

His source on the cruise ship had checked all the shore excursions the passengers had signed up for and discovered that Maeve Rivers had changed her plans and would not be going to Denali National Park after all. She was scheduled now to fly to Barrow instead.

Her daughter must have talked her into viewing the polar bears known to be gathering now on the edge of the Arctic Ocean up in Barrow. He imagined the little brat whining to her mother about polar bears all over the earth dying because of global warming and that it might be a 'now or never' opportunity to see them in one of their natural habitats before they became extinct.

This change of plans made everything much more convenient for him. What was the expression? 'Killing two birds with one stone.'

Professor Nicholson was becoming chronically sick of this whole matter and looked forward to finishing 'things' up soon and returning to his South African game reserve.

***

Interpol had alerted the cruise ship's security officers to be on lookout and posted the image of Mrs. Reginald Puce that Robert Rivers had extracted from the ship's formal dining room surveillance tape.

Even though there was an Interpol guard posted outside of Passenger Puce's door, the *Alaskan Sun* security officers immediately alerted their shore excursion staff to be on high alert and to detain a 'Mrs. Puce' if she tried to disembark at Icy Strait Point.

So far, according to the door cameras, there had only been a handful of elderly women passengers who had already disembarked and all of them had valid swipe keys.

After checking with room service, it seemed that Mrs. Reginald Puce had not ordered breakfast to be delivered to her stateroom. It should only be a matter of a short time until Puce left her room for a late breakfast or brunch. If she did not leave, Interpol would get a search warrant and do a room invasion. Mrs. Puce had thirty more minutes.

***

After Liffey had finally calmed Sinead down the night before and they had both gone to bed, she drifted in and out of a restless, half-awake state all night.

Had she really kissed John? True, it was not exactly a big deal. Nothing like a movie finale kiss. Yet a part of her still hoped that the ending scenario for them would be like Rose and Jack on the *Titanic* but without the iceberg and shipwreck.

She thought about trying to talk her mother out of the whale spotting tour she had booked for them later this morning and play tennis instead with the twins. It was worth a try.

***

"Liffey, do you think the lads will be going whale watching too?" Sinead asked hopefully over her bowl of cereal in the suite's dining room.

"Maybe. Who knows," Liffey answered gloomily.

She hated it when Sinead called boys 'lads.' It sounded old-fashioned and weird. It made her picture the twins wearing plaid kilts and long, woolen knee socks.

"Well we can find them again tonight at the club if it comes to that," Sinead continued, "and maybe even for another tennis lesson after we harpoon that great white whale, Moby Dick."

Liffey smiled. 'I wish I were as well-read as Sinead,' she thought. 'I bet that she and daddy are the only two people on this entire boat who have read *Moby-Dick*. I certainly haven't. I'll have to ask mother if she has.'

***

The three hour whale spotting tour put both Liffey and Sinead to sleep. After two hours of watching huge black and white flippers slapping at the water and spouts of water squirting up and then floating away like wisps of smoke as the water vaporized, they had both nodded off.

'I would bet that if this were five years ago, I would have had to restrain Liffey from diving overboard to swim with those whales,' Maeve thought ruefully. 'Now she can't stay awake for it. I missed so many of her wonder years.'

"Liffey and Sinead, wake yourselves up!" Maeve urged.

"You can put your ear to this hydrophone and hear the whales talking to each other."

"That's amazing," Liffey said without opening her eyes.

Sinead had begun to snore.

***

Interpol and Anderson detectives along with Robert Rivers and three officers from the *Alaskan Sun's* security staff used a master key to enter the stateroom of Mrs. Reginald Puce.

It was empty.

The bed had been stripped and there was no doubt that the whole room had been wiped clean of fingerprints.

The disappointed detectives began to do their forensic investigation in spite of the obvious fact that they were not going to find much, if anything at all.

Nothing was left in the stateroom that would provide so much as an atom of forensic evidence. Even the bed's spread and blankets and pillows were gone.

The room smelled heavily of cleaning fluid and bleach.

"He must have dumped everything overboard from his balcony last night," Louise said. "Stuffed everything he could into his luggage. I would bet he brought a hand-held vacuum cleaner along as well. This rug is spotless."

The attached clothes hangers in the closet were gone. The TV remote was missing. The couch slipcovers were gone.

"I've seen this kind of disappearing act before in Dublin," Eoin McGowan said when the McGowan brothers arrived.

"If our drug smugglers get a tip we are on to them, they will dump everything off shore before we get to them. It's very frustrating."

Michael McGowan added, "All they have to do is weight their stash down in a water tight container and send divers later to attach it to a boat and then pull it to shore when we've moved on to someone else."

"They either get a tip or have a very well developed sixth sense and can actually feel us coming after them," Eoin concluded.

"That man is always one step ahead of me," Robert Rivers said bitterly. "This time, I really thought we had him."

Interpol's project chief did not think it was over yet. "Where could this 'Mrs. Puce' go? It is, after all, Alaska, and it's not like it's easy blending in anonymously here like in some places. Let's find this guy before he leaves the state."

"The purser's officer on duty this morning told us that there were passengers who disembarked right at 9:00 a.m. when we docked," Louise said. "Our target is probably already gone. But at least I have already sent the dinner photo of Mrs. Puce to Hoonah airport."

"How did he manage to get off this ship so easily? He apparently knew he could no longer be 'Mrs. Puce' and obviously did not use Puce's swipe card. He had to have morphed into someone else with a valid identity card."

"But who?" a cluster of detectives muttered.

"And how?" a deflated Robert Rivers asked.

***

Liffey was looking at what had to be the world's biggest chicken wishbone. It was standing on the shoreline of an enormous body of icy water. Its bleached white bones reminded her of a miniature St. Louis Arch.

The wind picked up and dark storm clouds began to roll in to shore, casting dark shadows over the icy beach. Lightening zigzagged as the sky grew darker and thunder rumbled in the distance.

The scene switched to a polar bear climbing straight up the back side of a nearby ice hill. It was moving towards a man who did not see it closing in on him. The man stood perfectly still looking at a cell phone in his hand.

The bear reached the top of the ice hill and batted the man off it like a home run baseball hit. The man sailed far out into open waters and landed on an ice floe.

The white arch changed into a white whale. The whale turned into a white minivan and exploded.

The noise from the explosion woke Liffey up for a moment but when she realized it had only been a dream, she turned over and went back to sleep.

30

Professor Nicholson's plane landed in Anchorage, Alaska. He had almost missed his flight connection from Juneau, which would not have been good. He needed to maintain his head start.

He immediately left the airport and hailed a cab at the arrivals curb.

"8975 Iceberg Road, please."

The taxi cab driver nodded and, as if he were reading the professor's mind, floored the accelerator and sped away.

Ten minutes later, he saw a small, white RV parked in the driveway of a two-storey house across the street from the 8975 address.

He tipped the driver and when he saw the cab was out of sight, crossed the street to 8978 Iceberg Road. He opened the door of the used RV he had purchased last night while he was still on the *Alaskan Sun*. The money wire for $25,000 from a Chicago bank had been deposited into the RV seller's bank account overnight. He opened the glove box and was pleased that the title transfer document to the RV had been completed as he had requested. The RV title was signed over to 'Lionel Nicholson.'

He was not surprised that Interpol's phone surveillance had not picked up his own phone's outgoing calls. He had hired an ex-CIA communications specialist to scramble all his outgoing and any incoming calls he received. He had been able to order the plane tickets from Hoonah to Juneau and then from Juneau to Anchorage and even shop for the RV, by using his smart phone right under the noses of the detectives Robert Rivers had hired to chase after him.

Dr. Nicholson reached for the keys under the sun visor and set off for Barrow, Alaska, which on the map, looked like it was located at the very end of the earth.

Because the physical road to Barrow ended at a place called Deadhorse and he could not risk flying into the local Barrow airport, he would have to use another one of his multiple identities he had thought to bring along to enable him to reach his destination.

Deadhorse.

What an awful name for an outpost at the end of the earth.

A slight shiver passed over him and he heard his long dead grandmother telling him that if you "unexplainably shiver, it means that someone is walking on your grave."

He tried to ignore this memory and backed out of the driveway.

As he had instructed his purchasing agent, the RV came with a heater, CB radio, extra gasoline and was stocked with five days of food supplies and warm blankets and several gallons of bottled water. There was a small stove with three burners and dishes and utensils. He had brought along his own bag of ground Raven's Brew Coffee that he had picked up in a shop at the Hoonah airport before his twenty minute flight to Juneau. He had insisted that the RV have a coffee maker.

***

Dr. Nicholson calculated that he had a good head start. He was certain that he would be pursued and counted on the fact that the disguise he had worn disembarking the ship would keep his pursuers confused for hours, if not days.

He had worn a ski jacket and black skull cap as the temperature had been in the low 30's when he had set off from the *Alaskan Sun*. His oversized back pack made him look like an inquisitive tourist who was off to gather booklets and souvenirs. He had also worn cheap sun glasses and munched on a Danish to hide his cheekbones and mouth from surveillance cameras.

His pursuers might think that he had hired a private plane and perhaps had already left Alaska, defeated.

Attorney Rivers would think that he was discouraged now by his failed efforts to get to his daughter and wife. Rivers would feel relief that he was gone, but also some anxiety since he had once again failed to intercept the man who was stalking his little family.

It was true that he had hoped at first there might have been an opportunity to put an end to all this drama on the *Alaskan Sun*. But he knew it would be difficult, and he had thought from the very beginning of the cruise that he might have to travel up to Barrow and finish 'things' there.

It might make 'things' considerably more interesting for him to be hunting out of doors. It would be very much like stalking one of his lions on his reserve in Africa. Timing was everything with a lion. If you made a mistake, you might well be the lion's next meal.

Even though he had not been able to bag his quarry on the *Alaskan Sun*, his expert defensive reflexes had alerted him on the cruise ship's hunting ground that he himself was going to be bagged unless he fled.

Eventually he knew that his path would collide with his prey, quite possibly at an unexpected moment, and he was confident how it would all end.

***

The twins were nowhere to be seen when Liffey and Sinead returned to the *Alaskan Sun* after a quick tour of Hoonah.

Maeve suggested that now was a good time for her to observe the girls running through both their hard and soft shoe steps on the disco stage before they left port and they reluctantly agreed.

"We should have arranged to meet up with them today before we left the club last night, Liffey," Sinead griped moments later in their bedroom.

Sinead's bad mood was contagious. "You're probably right, Sinead, but we do not want to appear to be too anxious—like we're desperate and have nothing else to do," said Liffey.

"Well, Liffey, what else *do* we have to do?"

"Well for one thing, both of us need to practice lots more before the Anchorage Feis, Sinead."

"And let's face it, after this cruise is over, they go back to Rhode Island, you go back to Ireland and I go back to Wisconsin."

Sinead groaned, "But Liffey, I've never had so much fun."

Liffey had to agree. She could not think of one other night in her entire life when she had had so much fun either.

***

Liffey could not believe how hard her mother pushed them at Irish dance practices.

Scissors, quivers, clicks, butterflies, leapovers….

"Sinead, you need to watch your turnout and keep those arms DOWN at your side. You look like a chicken in a barnyard trying to fly."

"Liffey, keep your knees CROSSED and remember to breathe! You look like you're going to keel over!"

When Liffey reminded her mother that she was not exactly practicing for the World's, Maeve responded, "Oh yes you are!"

***

Aunt Jean had met a world adventurer at the lower deck's piano bar last night. She said he was a mountain climber and deep sea diver who had described many harrowing experiences to her in graphic detail.

"Liffey, one time when Kenneth was standing on the very summit of Mount McKinley, he became air born in a great gust of wind and had to body surf on the wind currents all the way down to the bottom of the mountain."

Liffey gave her aunt a skeptical look and said:

"That's impossible, Aunt Jean. It never happened. He was lying and trying to impress you."

"You are so wrong, Liffey. Ken told me that he is the president of the International Human Kite Association and he has speaking engagements all over the world."

"I have asked him to join me for dinner tonight as you and Sinead have indicated you would prefer to eat at the buffet instead of in the formal dining room."

"That's just great, Aunt Jean!" Liffey exclaimed with genuine delight. "Sinead and I will eat at the buffet and then you will have plenty of room for your guest."

"Would you like to know about his incredible diving mishap at the bottom of the Caspian Sea?"

"Absolutely, Aunt Jean. I will find you guys after the buffet and he can tell me all about what it's like to be incredible at the bottom of the Caspian Sea."

"Liffey, darling, where *is* the Caspian Sea?" Aunt Jean asked.

Liffey hesitated and then replied:

"Narnia."

Aunt Jean smiled and said, "Thanks, darling."

***

After several hours of interviewing the *Alaskan Sun* crew manning the disembarkation door, the Hoonah and Juneau airport employees and a call to the pilot of the morning plane from Hoonah to Juneau, nothing concrete had turned up.

The Hoonah flight to Juneau had been full and the six passengers on it had all connected to other flights. Interpol had been able to locate all but one of the six passengers—a Lionel Nicholson, who had flown to Anchorage and then vanished.

Lionel Nicholson was not a registered guest in any Anchorage hotels. There were no car rentals. Perhaps he was staying with some relatives while on business in Juneau.

The security camera in Hoonah at the airport check-in desk had a clear picture of Dr. L. Nicholson but no one who even remotely resembled him could be matched up with any of the male passengers who had left the cruise ship for a shore excursion. It seemed that Dr. Nicholson had not been on the *Alaskan Sun*.

Interpol reluctantly decided to pull out after their forensic technicians had not discovered so much as an eyelash or skin cell in the sanitized room where Mrs. Puce had stayed. There was nothing more to work with in Alaska and they had many other requests for assistance from all over the globe.

Robert Rivers understood Interpol's position. Their objective here had been to bring in a terrorist on a Most

Wanted list, not to protect the Rivers family. They could not justify any more time and expense here in Alaska.

Attorney Rivers was not at all convinced that his family was out of danger but he was determined to see the trip through. From Seward, they would travel to Anchorage for the feis and then to Barrow to see the polar bears.

Sheila Sullivan was going to fly home from Anchorage and begin a new assignment in Illinois.

He was certain that if Dr. Lionel Nicholson was their man and had somehow managed to fly undetected from Anchorage to Barrow, he would be discovered there tomorrow by the two Anderson detectives who were already on their way to Barrow from Juneau.

The detectives would first review all of the incoming flight arrival photos from the day before their arrival, and then monitor all incoming flights themselves thereafter.

And if, by some bad decision making, the Raven had decided to drive, there were no roads going all the way to Barrow. Only restricted, private roads along the shore of the Arctic Ocean which were owned by oil companies.

But no one in their right mind would attempt the drive north along the Dalton Highway, which was a dangerous gravel road much of the way, used only by trucks delivering supplies to oil companies.

Even if he did make it all the way to Deadhorse, he would then have to fly to Barrow and Barrow was already on high alert.

Deadhorse was a dead end.

31

"**H**ow are we supposed to know when the twins will be going to the buffet, Liffey? We can't just go in there and stuff our faces all night waiting to see if they turn up!"

"I think I could do that," Liffey laughed.

"I'm famished after that workout my mother just put us through."

"It was really nice of Aunt Jean to clear the way for us tonight, I'm not sure I could have looked my mother in the eye and told her that we wanted to eat at the buffet tonight without blushing. She would have totally guessed why."

"Do you think your aunt's friend really body surfed down from a mountain top on wind currents?"

"Sure. It's possible, Sinead."

Sinead looked surprised.

"Seriously? How?"

"If you're from another planet, like my Aunt Jean."

***

It was 8:00 p.m. when Liffey realized that she could not eat one more bite.

"Come on, Sinead. Let's get out of here before we both explode."

"No argument. It's pretty obvious they're not coming to graze here tonight."

"Besides, daddy wants a family meeting in about fifteen minutes in the suite."

"So he's making a speaker call?"

"No. He'll be speaking to us in the suite."

Sinead looked confused.

"Whatever. Let's ask your mum if we can go back to the club right after your dad's speech."

***

Robert Rivers approached the elevator slowly. He was apprehensive about how much to say about everything that had happened since the *Alaskan Sun* had left Vancouver.

Only Liffey knew that he had been on this cruise from the beginning, and he had asked her not to tell anyone.

Now that the danger had passed, at least for the moment, he thought that it was time to join his family while Louise and her detectives, along with the McGowan brothers, continued their vigilance.

He had decided not to tell Liffey yet about Sister Helen's phone call and the plan they had hatched together to welcome her little brother into the family.

There was also the delicate matter of telling Maeve that she had a son. He feared that the shock might be too much for her and bring on a relapse, but she had to know before she met Neil.

Attorney Rivers wondered how much endurance he himself had left to cope with this constant worrying about his family's safety and sanity. He was completely out of gas.

***

There was a stunned silence when Robert Rivers walked off the suite's elevator into the living room at 8:15 p.m.

"Well let's not all get too excited and overcome with emotion here, ladies," he joked.

Maeve was the first to react and ran over to him with a welcoming hug. "Robert! How wonderful to have you with us!"

Liffey was not sure how she should react since she already knew her father had been on board since they had left Vancouver.

"Daddy! It really is great to have you with us!"

"Yes, it really is, Mr. Rivers," said Sinead, giving Liffey an inquisitive 'is this good or not?' look.

"Robert, darling, you must try the salmon rolls, they're divine," was all Aunt Jean managed to say.

Sheila Sullivan had gone to bed early.

Tomorrow the *Alaskan Sun* would arrive at Juneau.

***

Liffey was wearing her favorite skinny jeans and lucky green sweater. Sinead followed Liffey's casual lead and combined black leggings with a soft blue pullover sweater, as they set off in high spirits for the Teen Scene.

"I think this was much easier before they paid so much attention to us, Liffey," Sinead said, wringing her hands together.

"I agree. Not expecting anything is way easier than hoping things will get even better."

"Well it's not our fault your mother dragged us off all day looking for whales. If the lads wanted to play tennis, at least they had their parents."

"Make sure you look totally surprised when the twins see us, Liffey. We cannot look all dithery. We need to look cool and composed."

170

"That's me, Sinead. Aloof Liffey. Really surprised to see that the boys are at the club too."

The Teen Scene was even darker than it had been the night before and after several minutes had elapsed and no one had come to claim them, Liffey said:

"Let's go in, Sinead. Maybe they're not even in there."

They made their way slowly through the crowd but before they reached the back wall where they had sat the night before, Sinead jerked to a stop and stared straight ahead like she had seen a ghost.

Liffey had trouble in the inky blackness making out exactly what it was that Sinead was looking at. She was squinting, trying to bring things into focus, when suddenly it felt like something had knocked the wind out of her. She swallowed hard, grabbed Sinead's hand and said, "Let's get out of here, it looks like we were not expected after all."

Two blondes with Atomic pink highlights, eyes heavy with black mascara and lips redder than Heinz Ketchup, were seated at last night's table with the twins. The girls were laughing hysterically and one of them was applying a moustache to one of the twins with a mascara brush. Both of the twins wore stupid smiles on their faces.

Sinead brushed a few tears she could not hold back from the bridge of her nose and removed Liffey's clenched hand.

"No, Liffey. You and I are not going anywhere. Let's find a table on the other side of the room. Do you want us to have to play twenty questions with your mum about why we came back from the club so early?"

"No. I guess not," Liffey said, even though she really *did* want to go back to the suite and throw herself into the comforting arms of her mother and sob.

"I know the lads are not exactly out scouting for us, but I just can't face going back to the suite yet," Sinead said, wiping another column of tears from her cheeks with the back of her hand.

"Neither can I," Liffey said flatly.

"Maybe we really should leave, Liffey?"

This time, it was Liffey who disagreed. She led Sinead over to a table near the stage where two young women were setting up to perform. A placard identified them as the WILLIAMS SISTERS.

"If they had bagpipes and a tin whistle, instead of a guitar and keyboard, I would ask them to play a lament for us, Liffey."

"Play a what?"

"A lament. It's sad, moaning music that's played when people are grieving about something they've lost, like a battle or lost love," Sinead said, as the two performers sat down with their guitar and keyboard and began to sing:

> *Drowning in the depths of the river*
> *Ever haunted by your face*
> *Craving for that feeling familiar*
> *That my heart and fingers traced*
> *If I had something to tell you*
> *Would you ever find the time?*
> *Cause that was the past and*
> *I took the last stand*
> *You were the fool…*

"It's our *Alaskan Sun* lament," Sinead sighed.

"Let's go," both girls said simultaneously.

32

Professor Nicholson was energized by the Alaskan midnight sun as he approached the city of Fairbanks.

It had been a long, eight hour drive from Anchorage in his slow RV but it was still light and would be for many hours to come.

After he crossed the Arctic Circle at the 115 Mile Post on the Dalton Highway north of Fairbanks, the sun would not set for the next three months.

Perhaps he would not have to sleep all the way to Deadhorse. Like some of the other great men in history, he needed very little sleep. Napoleon and Thomas Jefferson only slept for two hours each day. He only slept four.

Even though he knew that many people might find his line of work offensive, he still thought of himself as an important person in the big scheme of things. Occasionally, it was necessary to make difficult decisions such as ending a life or two when such lives threatened his existence. All great men did that. Many of those men were labeled heroes.

He did not look at himself as a hero, but he was a very successful entrepreneur. Many of his underlings were now wealthy because of his business expertise.

He had five more days to leisurely drive north. Perhaps he would pan for gold like a tourist along the Dalton Highway. Since the sun would not be setting, he could take his time and have some fun for a change. Daydream about the loud explosion to come and living in a world without Liffey Rivers while he sifted for nuggets along a roadside stream.

***

"I don't know how much more of this beautiful scenery I can take, Liffey," Sinead said, leaning over the suite's balcony, sipping orange juice while the snow-capped mountain shoreline passed by.

"I mean, how much stunning scenery can one person cope with day after day?"

Liffey agreed. "I feel like we're all living in a travel brochure. Everything along this Inner Passage is too picture perfect. Maybe panning for gold later on today, we'll get all muddy and dirty and begin to feel like real people again."

"And speaking of getting real, we need to practice our steps. I am not feeling very confident about dancing for real in a few days."

Sinead sighed.

"I'll ask my mom if she feels up to it and we'll take it from there," Liffey decided.

"Do you think we'll find any gold, Liffey? I'd love to find a nugget and have it set in a pendant for my mum."

"You can have anything I find. My mother likes silver. She says the King Midas story scared her to death when she was little because he wished that everything he touched would turn to gold and then forgot and hugged his poor little daughter by mistake..."

"And she turned into a golden statue," Sinead finished the story. "Speaking of golden people, I wonder if we'll see the twins today, Liffey?"

"I hope not," Liffey said curtly. "I'll make sure to bring some creek slime back with us and fling it at them if we do!"

***

"This is way more fun than pawing through the lumpy sand at Streedagh Strand in Sligo looking for Spanish gold doubloons, and never finding one," Sinead said, dipping her pan into the stream and swirling the dirty water in a circular motion to allow everything to settle on the bottom.

Liffey felt a wave of panic. Sinead had just unwittingly opened the door for her father to begin another boring history lecture.

It was too late. Before Liffey could think of something fast enough to detour her father from the history lesson she could see percolating in his head, he began:

"Ah, Streedagh Strand. The place where three Spanish Armada ships wrecked in 1588. Sad story, that. Over a thousand of the Spanish made it to shore alive, but once there, all but a handful were murdered by the English under Richard Bingham…"

After fifteen minutes of what Liffey had to admit was a grim but fascinating story, he was done. Was her father becoming much more interesting? Or was she beginning to tolerate or worse, maybe even *like* his history sermons? She hoped not.

She was crouched down in the ankle high stream in her rubber rental boots, scooping up creek bottom mud, when she felt something like an electric current moving from her fingertips up to her elbows.

She jumped up and looked closely at her father and Sinead. Neither of them looked like they were experiencing anything uncomfortable which was unsettling.

She dipped her sieve underwater again and this time, the electric pins and needle sensations were unmistakable.

'Am I imagining this? Or is this a warning?'

***

Professor Nicholson was bent over with a large sluice box, sifting for gold in a shallow tributary of the Yukon River.

Leisurely prospecting for gold in this small stream right off the Dalton Highway, he was daydreaming about what it must have been like a hundred years ago when miners were staking gold claims in Alaska hoping to strike it rich.

He carefully extracted a small fragment of gold from the prospecting box, and decided it was time to move on.

***

Later in the suite, Liffey printed out a map of the Yukon River. Tracing it, she could see that it flowed all the way from western Canada up into Alaska and then down again, making a lopsided semicircle.

It intersected with the Dalton Highway north of Fairbanks and a large network of tributaries from the river extended as far down as Juneau, where she had been prospecting for gold earlier today.

Liffey felt whiplashed when she realized that the Skunk Man must have been standing in a connecting river or creek today at the same time she had been in her stream, and that the electric sensations she had felt were because of him.

Had he been fishing?

Panning for gold like her?

What was it that her father was always saying about reality? "Everything on this earth is interconnected, Liffey, but most of us do not have the sensitivity to recognize it."

She hated thinking about ruining her father's good mood which she knew she would when she told him that they might still be in grave danger.

She also hated knowing that when she did manage to get her nerve up and tell him, they would be pretty much stuck on the ship until they reached Seward.

33

Robert Rivers woke everybody up at 7:00 a.m. and ushered them out on to the balcony. The *Alaskan Sun* was docking in Skagway.

Aunt Jean was alarmed.

"Does this ship have wheels, Robert? It looks like we are about to go right down Main Street!"

He drew in a deep breath of pristine Alaskan air and said, "I smell breakfast, ladies, let's go find something to eat and get our strength up. You never know, we might be needed to help push this boat back into the water."

"Who's coming to the buffet with me?"

Liffey and Sinead exchanged nervous glances and followed. Aunt Jean went back to bed. Maeve and Sheila opted for Room Service so they could finish the latest books they were reading.

"So, have you girls managed to meet any one on board your own age?" Robert Rivers inquired in the elevator with an 'I already know the answer to this question' look.

"I am guessing you would already *know* we have, Daddy," Liffey answered slowly, fully expecting him to bring up the twins. But before he could begin his usual cross-examination, she blurted out: "Daddy, I had the pins and needles warning yesterday while I was standing in the stream. I think he's still here in Alaska."

"Why did you wait this long to tell me, Liffey? This is serious."

"I didn't know how to bring it up. It always sounds crazy when I talk about the pins and needles and I…"

Her father interrupted her: "Liffey, you know well that I believe in your internal alarm system. I'll need to talk with Louise and the McGowan brothers immediately so they can regroup."

"The *McGowan* brothers, Mr. Rivers?" Sinead looked baffled.

Robert Rivers immediately realized he had slipped up.

"I suppose it won't do any harm now for you to know that both of your brothers are part of my surveillance and protection staff on this cruise, Sinead."

"Louise and Interpol are overloaded keeping track of Liffey's and Maeve's every move."

"Interpol? Like in spy movies, Mr. Rivers?"

"Yes. Interpol like in spy movies, was initially involved, Sinead."

"So why then would you need my brothers here?"

"Their primary function is to keep you safe, Sinead. The other detectives already had their hands full. Your brothers' responsibility is you—only you. For instance, yesterday, in Juneau, Eoin and Michael were in the gold mine we toured and they sat up in trees along the stream afterwards with binoculars when were panning for gold."

"Why are you talking about Interpol in the past tense now, Daddy?" Liffey asked.

"Unfortunately, when our target caught on that we were on to him, he vanished. Just disappeared. Interpol could not justify staying on. They put out alerts at all

Canadian border checks but it's unlikely they'll bring him in that way."

"In the meantime, we have to assume he will come back at us and we must remain on high alert. I am still convinced we are going to bring him in on this trip."

"I'll be back soon," Robert Rivers said abruptly leaving them in the breakfast buffet line.

Liffey's eyes swept through the dining room.

"They're not in here, Sinead. I'm hungry. Let's eat. If we are not going to be allowed to go into Skagway today, we might as well make the best of it."

"I still have the two books I brought along to read."

***

"What's happened to the twins?" Maeve asked out of the blue when the girls returned to the suite.

Liffey often suspected that her mother was a mind-reader and had been waiting for her to ask this question.

"What twins?"

"What do you mean, *what* twins?" Maeve said.

Her mother was obviously not going to gracefully drop this painful subject so Liffey answered honestly:

"They dumped us."

"What do you mean 'dumped' you? I thought they were helping you play tennis?"

Sinead barged in. "Oh they *were* helping us with our tennis, Mrs. Rivers, but then we saw them in the club that night and they kissed us."

Liffey blushed and shot Sinead an exasperated '*please* don't make this any worse than it already is' look.

"I mean we kissed them back too but…"

Maeve tried not to look amused when she saw the horrified look on Liffey's face and broke in:

"Liffey, I don't expect you to tell me all the details but I would think that a first kiss might be something you might want to at least mention?"

"That is, assuming it was your first kiss?"

Liffey was indignant.

"Yes, mother, it was. But we haven't even talked with them since. They were with two other girls when we went back to the club again."

Liffey fervently hoped that her mother was going to drop this unpleasant conversation.

"Well, it's their loss," Maeve stated like this was obvious.

"I say both of you get your dancing gear together right now and we'll go down to our stage for some practice."

"Sounds good to me," Sinead said. "I wonder if my brothers will be lurking around. I don't think they've seen me dance since I was seven."

"Well then, they're in for a big surprise, aren't they?" Maeve said.

Sinead giggled and said, 'Thanks to you, Mrs. Rivers."

Liffey forced a faint 'I agree' smile and nodded.

'How could Sinead have said all those horrible things to someone's *mother*?'

***

Liffey could hardly breathe when she finished her slip jig but Maeve Rivers did not seem to notice.

"Let's change into your hard shoes now. We'll begin with your treble jigs."

Eoin McGowan set down his bucket of cleaning supplies and stopped outside the door when the hornpipe music began. Michael McGowan, who was wiping smears and sticky fingerprints from the hall's paneled walls while he surveyed the passing traffic, joined his brother.

A small crowd began to gather at the door. Some of them began to clap in time to the rhythm of the pounding feet from inside. Liffey and Sinead were oblivious.

The hypnotized crowd in the doorway grew larger. Liffey and Sinead were concentrating so intensely that they were unaware they had attracted an audience. The clapping in the doorway blended in with the claps of foot-thunder echoing off the stage floor.

When Maeve turned the music off, loud applause came from the hallway. Startled, Liffey and Sinead managed to catch their breath, smile, and wave.

Hands waved back at them.

Four of them belonged to the twins.

"Liffey, what are we going to do?" Sinead mumbled frantically.

"About what?" answered Liffey, trying to catch her breath.

"What do you mean about *what*? About the twins out there looking in at us!"

"We're not going to *do* anything. Why should we?"

Maeve gave Liffey a 'way to go' nod and said:

"Would you girls like to join me now to meet up with Jean and Sheila in the small theatre? We're going to a short film and twenty minute lecture about the Hubbard Glacier. Since we obviously cannot dock there tomorrow and will have to stay on the ship to view it, I think it would be a good idea to know something about it beforehand, don't you?"

Liffey said, "Absolutely. I'm in. Let's go!"

Sinead hesitated. The twins were clearly out in the hallway waiting for her and Liffey. She tried to hide her noticeable disappointment and reluctantly agreed.

"Good. Let's go eat some Dip'n'Dots to lower our body temperatures before we watch the ice movie," Maeve said.

"You didn't tell us you were Irish dancers," one of the twins said to the group as it left their practice area. Liffey was almost sure it was John but was not 100% certain. This identical twin thing was not easy.

"You didn't ask," Liffey answered coldly.

"Why don't you join us for some tennis?" the other twin said.

Before Liffey realized that she was actually turning down their invitation to play tennis, she heard herself replying, "No thanks. We're going to a lecture and short film after we lower our body temperatures."

Both twins gave them a quizzical look.

Maeve nodded and quickly added, "But another tennis lesson would be good for the girls if it's convenient for them."

"See you around then," Liffey said.

Sinead went limp with disappointment. She was well aware that Maeve and Liffey were giving the twins a dose of their own medicine. She wished she had the courage to join in with them and say something lighthearted, but she was too distracted trying not to cry.

***

Sister Helen was making final preparations. She had never left the Home for more than a few days before and there was still much to be done if she was going to be gone for two whole weeks.

Neil kept busy walking with his cane and reading travel books and online brochures about America. He had never been out of South Africa before and now it felt like he was going to another planet. As long as he could eat his Jungle

Oats cereal for breakfast every morning, he was confident things would work out.

***

This so-called Dalton Highway was a joke. 'How can this disaster be called a road? It's more like a dirt bike trail.'

Professor Nicholson was exasperated. He was sick and tired of avoiding deep potholes and traveling at only forty miles per hour and sometimes less. At this rate, it was going to be difficult, if not impossible for him to reach Barrow in time for the Rivers' polar bear expedition.

He needed to pick up his pace.

***

"Ladies and gentlemen, we will see the Hubbard Glacier calving tomorrow morning," the lecturer said, animatedly pointing his long stick at the projection screen. "You will witness chunks of ice as high as ten stories detaching, or calving, from this magnificent glacier. After calving, these floating masses of ice are called icebergs."

"If glaciers have calves, Liffey, then what do cows have?" Sinead whispered.

"Ice cream?" Liffey suggested.

"I dare you to ask Professor Shiver up there that question after the movie's over," Liffey whispered, sincerely hoping that Sinead was not going to start convulsing with laughter and drag her into it again.

"I think I'll ask your aunt instead, Liffey. Her answer would probably be way more interesting than anything our glacier expert up there might have to say."

Liffey tried unsuccessfully to suppress the laughter she felt rising up inside her. Trying to imagine what her Aunt Jean would have to say about glacier calving reminded her of the time on safari when Aunt Jean had told her with a straight face that a black mamb'o' snake could collapse its jaws and swallow a whole cape buffalo.

Sinead was holding her hands over her mouth when she jumped up and rushed out from the last row of seats in the theatre, followed by Liffey who collapsed into a heap with her on the floor outside the door.

"What happens when a cow laughs too hard?"

Liffey tried to answer but was laughing too hard.

"It Cowlapses!"

"What is *WRONG* with those girls?" Eoin McGowan complained to his brother, looking over his clipboard from a table in the snack bar across from the theatre. They were both wearing *Alaskan Sun* officers' uniforms again, trying to blend in with a group of high school students on a class trip.

"It just never gets any better with them."

***

The girls were still sitting against the wall in the hallway just outside the auditorium door, eyes closed, roaring with laughter, when they were interrupted:

"What's so funny?" asked a familiar voice. It belonged to John.

Another voice echoed, "Yes, what's so funny?"

Liffey opened one eye slowly and said, "I thought you were playing tennis?"

"We were planning to until you guilt-tripped us into doing something intellectual for a change. From the state of both of you, I am guessing that the brainy life's not easy for you either."

Liffey almost snapped something snooty back at him but realized she had little ground to stand on here since the twins *had* caught her sneaking out of the lecture theatre and then, howling in a pile on the floor.

"It's just, I mean, we were doing fine in there until he pointed at the glacier in the film and said it was calving and Sinead asked me that if glaciers have calves, then what do

184

cows have, and…well, we had to get out of there before we were being obviously disrespectful," Liffey explained as she stood up and hauled Sinead back up on her feet.

"Well, I'm glad we came," said John, "because now there's no way we're going to sleep through that glacier show tomorrow morning. Can you meet us in the buffet for breakfast? We promised our parents we'd wear the sport jackets they made us bring and eat in the formal dining room tonight with them. They also guilt-tripped us into playing doubles with them after dinner."

Before Sinead could reply, Liffey said:

"Knock, Knock"

"Who's there?"

"Alaska."

"Alaska who?"

"Alaska my mother if we can come
out tomorrow and play."

John moaned. "You warned me you could do worse!"

Eoin McGowan also moaned. "It's those tennis jocks again, and that has to be the stupidest Knock Knock joke I've ever heard."

***

"Liffey, how does your clueless aunt manage to beat all of us at *Scrabble* every time we play it? I'm seriously interested," Sinead commented, after Jean Rivers had won three games in a row.

"I mean, it seems like she doesn't have a thought in her head and then she routinely trounces all of us."

"I have no idea how she does it," Liffey answered. "Every time I think Aunt Jean is totally blank, she'll say or do something totally smart. I've stopped trying to analyze her because it makes me crazy."

"I thought that her final answer after we all discussed tomorrow's glacier calving and whether or not cows can birth ice cream if glaciers can have calves was brilliant, Liffey."

"How did she put it again? Something like if a black mamb'o' can swallow a cape buffalo, then anything on this earth is possible."

Liffey nodded and said, "That's correct."

"By the way," Sinead continued, "What do you call a cow that has just had a calf?"

"I give up," Liffey said.

"Decalfinated."

34

L iffey put down her binoculars and went back inside the suite to find warm clothing for a morning on the deck after breakfast.

It was 6:00 a.m.

Even though Sinead had been almost hyperventilating yesterday, after the twins had invited them to breakfast this morning, she was still fast asleep.

"Sinead, wake up!" Liffey yelled from the doorway.

Sinead rolled out of bed on to the floor with a shrill cry: "*Please* don't tell me we've overslept and missed our balanced breakfast, Liffey!"

***

Liffey could not decide what was most thrilling: eating a large jelly donut without being admonished by Aunt Jean or her mother about trans fats, looking at the far off wall of blue glacial ice which seemed to have no beginning or end, or eating breakfast with John, who it turned out was not just a tennis jock. He had brought along high powered binoculars and an extra pair of sunglasses for Liffey so she could comfortably stare at the twinkling ice.

After both of them had finished their yogurts, apples, bananas, donuts, and hot chocolate, he took Liffey by the hand and led her out on to the deck to listen to the calving noises the glacier was making as huge pieces of it split off, and the newly-calved icebergs crashed into the water.

Sometimes it sounded like rolling thunder with booms and bangs.

Other times, it sounded like a shot gun was being fired off in the distance. Sometimes it just creaked and moaned.

John explained that the haunting blue color of the glacier was created by the density of the ice.

"The dense ice absorbs all the colors of the spectrum except?"

"Anyone?"

Liffey got the clue: "Except *blue*."

"Correct. You're a genius! The color blue is reflected."

"By the way, you are an amazing Irish dancer. My older sister used to do that. She quit after she started college."

Liffey suddenly realized that she had never asked the twins what their last name was, or if they had any other siblings.

"Are you Irish then?"

"How does O'Toole sound to you?"

"Seriously?"

"No. How about O'Malley?"

"Really?"

"No."

"How about O'Leary?"

"Honestly?"

Liffey began to laugh and handed the binoculars back to John.

It was like the entire shoreline had turned into a sparkling blue diamond in the early morning sun.

She was sorry this was the last day of their in-bound cruise. Tomorrow morning at 4:00 a.m., the *Alaskan Sun* would dock at Seward and she would be off to the Anchorage Feis.

This meant that she would have to get a full, good night's sleep or pay the consequences at the feis. It also meant that now that she could finally tell John apart from Luke, their time together was going to be over all too soon.

✳✳✳

"I think we've finally lost them!" Sinead called out as she and Luke came running over to Liffey and John.

Luke looked relieved.

"I *told* you we have bodyguards!" Sinead said loudly.

Liffey froze. Surely Sinead had not told Luke about the Skunk Man?

John looked bewildered.

"Bodyguards?"

Liffey instinctively knew that major damage control had to happen right now if she were going to have any kind of normal last day on the *Alaskan Sun*.

"So you *had* to tell him we have bodyguards, Sinead?"

Sinead looked worried and embarrassed.

"You just had to tell him my father is breaking in new detectives for his agency, and we're the lucky specimens they get to follow around today while they're in training?"

Sinead looked stricken when it dawned on her that she had thoughtlessly exposed Liffey.

To her it had just seemed like a game of dodging her brothers.

"Oh well," said John, sensing that Sinead had done something way out-of-line, "for a minute there I thought maybe you two were famous."

Liffey smiled weakly.

"No. I'm afraid we're not."

Liffey could tell John was not buying her explanation of the bodyguards when he gave her hand a reassuring squeeze.

***

Liffey could not believe her ears. She had not yet recovered from the shock of Sinead's indiscretion when she heard a familiar voice coming from deep inside the crowd of glacier watchers: "Yoo Hoo! Liffey, darling!"

Things were about to get worse.

Aunt Jean had spotted her and was moving towards them with the telescope from their suite's balcony. The large fur hat with flaps she had purchased in Ketchikan was on her head and goggles covered her eyes. She looked like some kind of old-fashioned aviator in a soundless black and white movie. She looked ridiculous even for Aunt Jean.

"Liffey, darling! Sinead, dear! Here you both are!"

Liffey tried not to visibly flinch.

"Good morning, Aunt Jean. Yes, here we all are. Might I ask why you are wearing those goggles?"

"I am wearing these goggles to protect my eyes from sharp ice fragments, Liffey. You need more than those sun glasses, you know."

"But Aunt Jean, we are at least a third of a mile away from the glacier."

Aunt Jean ignored this observation and continued, "I have been watching the glacier for over an hour now, Liffey, and I think I can reassure you, with some authority, that the glacier is *not* going to have a calf."

Liffey wanted to jump overboard except that John's hand had tightened around hers and she could feel him trembling with suppressed laughter.

"I'm Harry Potter, Jean," John said, presenting his hand. "Pleased to make your acquaintance."

Aunt Jean glowed with approval, extended her own hand and said, "Your name sounds familiar, have we met before?"

'Welcome to my world, John,' Liffey heaved a sigh.

While Liffey was desperately plotting how to get her Aunt Jean to leave the vicinity without hurting her feelings, things continued to worsen.

"Jean! Is that you, dear?" a male voice called from a less crowded part of the viewing deck.

"Girls, it's Kenneth," Aunt Jean said breathlessly.

"You're finally going to meet him. He is the one who convinced me that cows *cannot* give birth to ice cream."

"*What* is she talking about?" John muttered under his breath. "Is she serious? Doesn't she get it that the whole calving thing was just a lame joke?"

"Nope, she takes everything everybody says literally."

Watching Kenneth making his way through the other glacier groupies with a permanent, fixed smile on his face, Liffey began to think about the scene from *Titanic* when Jack saved Rose from hurling herself into the ocean.

When she saw that her parents were now also walking towards her like a pair of deranged stalkers who had just cornered their victim, she wondered whether John would save her now if she stood up on the railing like Rose had done in *Titanic* and screamed at everybody to: "KEEP AWAY!"

35

P rofessor Nicholson estimated that he had at least one more full day of monotonous driving until he would finally arrive in Deadhorse, Alaska.

When he got there, he would become Chief Executive Officer 'Thomas T. Fields,' of the T. Fields & Sons Oil Company.

After shaving off all his hair, coloring his eyebrows auburn and applying glasses with dark, heavy frames that drew attention away from his face, he would sleep for the final time in his comfortable RV. The next morning, a corporate helicopter would transport him from Deadhorse to the oil fields his holding company had recently acquired near Barrow, Alaska.

He would quickly survey his new oil field acquisitions and thereafter be helicoptered back to Barrow to pick up the other vehicle he had purchased online. Then he would locate Liffey Rivers using a GPS signal and follow her van around looking for polar bears.

He regretted that it would be necessary to torch his comfortable RV before the arrival of the Fields' corporate helicopter.

Liffey was determined to make at least one point in her last doubles tennis match against Luke and Sinead. So far, John had made all of theirs.

Just when she thought it was hopeless, a ball sailed right at her and she hit it back before she realized what had happened.

"That's game, set and match!" John shouted. "Way to go, Liffey!"

Liffey was amazed at how smoothly things were going today--in spite of being in the company of her Aunt Jean, Kenneth, and her parents all morning long after the glacier viewing.

"John, Sinead and I have to practice our steps again for the feis tomorrow but my mother said to invite you and your family for a farewell dinner in our suite tonight," Liffey said, gathering up the extra tennis balls to return to the rental office.

"Won't we be a bit crowded?" John asked, handing her a ball hopper.

Sinead tossed a few balls at Liffey and snorted, "Oh, I think we'll all fit. What do you think, Liffey?"

Liffey agreed with Sinead and answered, "I think we'll all fit perfectly. And bring along that portable putt-putt golf game you told me about. My dad would love to show off his putting."

"Seriously? We can play golf in your suite?"

"Yes. And bring your bathing suits too so we can go into the hot tub out on our deck one last time."

"You have your own deck?" John looked confused.

"We have the owner's suite," Liffey finally confessed, "and I am pretty sure that they thought of everything."

Sinead had nothing to add.

After a two hour practice on the sprung stage in the disco, Maeve announced that she was confident Liffey and Sinead were ready for the Anchorage Feis in the morning.

"Let's go now and get the suite ready for our first and last company on the *Alaskan Sun*," said Maeve. "Also, I deliberately 'forgot' to tell both of you that Aunt Jean has invited her friend Kenneth tonight and he is going to present a short video about his experiences in the Sahara and Gobi deserts."

"You *are* kidding, right?" Liffey said, hoping she might have heard wrong.

"Afraid not, Liffey. Your aunt was so excited, I did not have the heart to tell her Kenneth should not bring his video. She said it's only ten minutes long and is very artistically done. Like the kind of short film that would play at a film festival."

Liffey was definitely disturbed. Aunt Jean's artistic taste was questionable, to put it mildly. Once, when her aunt was home schooling Liffey using the 'School of Life' technique she had developed, Liffey had spent seven hours watching *America's Next Top Model* episodes before her aunt switched to *Project Runway* reruns.

Liffey knew for a fact that Aunt Jean never watched any television unless it was some current brainless reality show, or a sitcom from the sixties like *I Dream of Jeannie* or *Petticoat Junction*. The only movie her aunt had ever talked about at length was something called *Gidget Goes to Rome*.

"Well I'm afraid it's a done deal, girls. This means a lot to Aunt Jean and I am sure you will both give her the respect she deserves during Kenneth's presentation. By that, I mean no running out of the room holding your hands over your mouths to stifle your hilarity."

"By the way," Liffey asked, "how come people can't starve to death in the desert?"

Liffey looked from Maeve to Sinead. Both of them shrugged.

"Anyone?" They shrugged again.

"Because of all the sand which is there!"

***

After everyone had enjoyed the sesame crusted Alaskan halibut and an array of other Alaskan delicacies presented in the formal dining room in the Rivers' suite, Aunt Jean announced that it was "show time."

Before anyone could comment, she handed each of the diners a pair of inexpensive goggles like the ones she had worn to watch the glacier calving to "set the mood," and beckoned everyone over to the large screen television to watch Kenneth's movie, *Desert Heat*.

Liffey did not risk looking at Sinead or John or Luke for fear of howling uncontrollably again which would irk her mother. They had been warned.

She put on her goggles and sat down on one of the Chinese Modern upholstered chairs which Kenneth had turned facing the television. John sat down in the chair next to hers which was not good for laughter control. She was afraid to even glance sideways at him because any eye contact whatsoever would be too risky.

Suddenly a spotlight went on in the room, making it uncomfortably bright. The rest of the audience put on their tinted goggles and Kenneth pressed 'Play.'

Ten minutes of watching blowing sand followed. Some of the sand eventually formed dunes. Other gusts of sand turned the atmosphere orange and blotted out the sun. There was no soundtrack. No voiceover. Just ten minutes of blowing sand.

When the screen went dark, Aunt Jean began to clap wildly. Liffey was still afraid to look at anyone, or for that matter, move away from her seat. She began to clap enthusiastically like her aunt to circumvent the giggles she could feel beginning to bubble up from her stomach.

Somehow, Liffey and Sinead and the twins made it out on to the balcony before they removed their goggles and exploded with pent-up laughter.

"It looked to me like he made the whole thing with his phone camera," Luke finally managed to say.

"I think he went googling and lifted all of it online," Liffey offered.

"I think it's time for some midnight sun and the hot tub," Sinead said seriously. "I need to get all this sand off me."

***

At ten o'clock Maeve announced the inevitable.

"I cannot believe this evening has gone by so quickly. I truly wish we did not have to get up at 3:00 a.m. to be ready for early departure when we arrive at Seward at 4:00 a.m. But if we miss the train to Anchorage, the girls won't be able to dance because there's no way we can drive safely on unfamiliar roads with so little sleep and the girls still have to eat a small plate of spaghetti and meatballs before they go to bed. Room Service should be delivering it any minute."

John gave Liffey a quizzical look. She blushed and explained: "If we don't eat spaghetti and meatballs the night before we dance, it's not good."

John asked politely, "Exactly what is it that would happen to you if you did not eat your magic noodles?"

"I don't exactly know because I've never risked it."

"So you're crazy then? I suspected this might be the case," John said, shaking his head with mock sadness. "Maybe I can help you?"

Liffey smiled and said, "You could certainly try."

"We've had a great time. Thanks so much. We must keep in touch," the twins' parents, Colette and Thomas Bergman, said politely.

Liffey was afraid she was going to cry. She had never expected to spend so much time with a boy she actually liked so much. John was different. He had explained he had not seen her that night in the Teen Scene when she had almost written him off, and that he had been hoping she was going to come. He said he and his brother had been harassed by the two blondes all night and that one of them had spent most of the night texting her boyfriend.

"We were waiting for you to come and save us but when you never turned up, we finally just escaped. Do you really think I would have ignored you?"

Liffey believed him, but now it was all over and she would probably never see him again.

The twins left with their parents.

Liffey and Sinead ate their spaghetti and meatballs. Then they pulled down the heavy shades in their room to block out the endless light in the land of the midnight sun.

***

At 3:50 a.m. the Rivers entourage made two trips down to the lobby in their private elevator. They had already arrived at Seward where they would take the shuttle to the train station.

At the departure ramp, Liffey was struggling to remain awake after only four hours of sleep when she felt a hand tap her on the shoulder from behind. She turned around and looked into John's deep blue eyes. The tears she had managed to fight off the night before began to run down her cheeks as he guided her face to his lips to say farewell. He kissed her lightly again right in front of her surprised parents and said, "I'll text you later. This is not good-bye, Liffey Rivers." Then he turned around and was gone.

"Oh my," Aunt Jean exclaimed, "how sweet!"

Robert Rivers looked anxiously at his wife. "Isn't this, a little too soon for this kind of thing?"

Maeve said consolingly, "She's fourteen now, Robert, and John seems to be very nice. But rest assured that I will certainly be monitoring the situation."

"I guess Luke's still sleeping. The eejit," Sinead said enviously.

***

The McGowan brothers were already off the *Alaskan Sun*, dressed as tourists in matching whale sweatshirts, ski caps and over-sized sunglasses.

They were sitting on the shuttle bus watching and waiting for Sinead and the others to board.

Even though they had been informed by Robert Rivers that Sinead now knew they were watching over her, they were resolved to keep a professional distance and do their job properly.

Louise Anderson and three of her detectives were already on their way to Anchorage where they would station themselves throughout the Anchorage Feis hotel.

The two Anderson detectives already onsite in Barrow at the airport, were almost certain that there had been no suspicious arrivals, before or after they had arrived.

They had conferred with the local police and were assured of their cooperation should they need it.

Louise was still hoping the homicidal maniac pursuing Liffey would turn up and that there would soon be an end to the constant uncertainty and upheaval in her young friend's life.

She had not yet told Robert Rivers that her office in St. Louis had received an untraceable envelope containing a black feather yesterday.

It had been driven for identification to the National Great Rivers Museum in nearby Illinois where there was a 'Masters of the Sky' bird exhibit.

The exhibit's curator had positively identified it.

The feather belonged to *Corvus Corax*—the Common Raven.

36

The gentle swaying of the early morning train as it hummed along the railroad tracks to Anchorage, had lulled everyone but Maeve and Sheila to sleep.

Sheila would be leaving them later today, after the Anchorage Feis, on an early evening flight to Chicago.

"It's really too bad everybody else is conked out and missing all of this beautiful scenery," Maeve commented over her shoulder while she gazed out her window at a shimmering turquoise-blue lake.

"I read somewhere that this train ride between Seward and Anchorage probably has the best scenery in the entire state," said Sheila from the seat directly in back of Maeve.

The train sped through dramatic mountain passes with unspoiled forests and rocky hillsides dotted with sheep. It descended into a deep canyon next to a large body of tidal water with waves crashing onto the shore.

"We saw the picture frame of all this as we sailed down the Inner Passage but now we're right in the middle of this gorgeous painting and they're *sleeping!* If the girls were not going to be dancing in a few more hours, I would pry their eyes open so they would not be missing this breathtaking landscape. Robert is completely bushed and it's far too risky waking Jean up from a sound sleep. She's like an irritable toddler if you do."

Maeve turned her head to smile at Sheila who had not responded to this latest conversation, but she too was now fast asleep.

Two hours later the conductor passed through the train car and called out in a singsong voice that they would be arriving in Anchorage in twenty minutes. When no one reacted, Maeve waited a bit before sounding her own ten minute warning.

Everyone but Sinead and Liffey managed to open their eyes.

"Let them have their final minutes," Maeve, Robert said gently. "They probably need them. I could certainly use some more sleep myself."

***

The feis hotel was only a five minute trip by taxi and Maeve had everybody settled in quickly. "I'm going downstairs to scope out the place, Liffey. When I get back, I expect you and Sinead to be stretched, dressed and wigged."

Aunt Jean walked through the door as Maeve left. She began stretching with the girls, and confided that she was downcast because there was no adult dancer competition here at this feis. She explained that she was afraid she might become "clinically depressed" if she came along to watch them dance and could not risk it.

Liffey was greatly relieved. Although her aunt had managed to surprise her once in a while at a feis and behave almost normally, Liffey knew from experience that Aunt Jean was likely to do something totally flaky and sometimes terminally embarrassing.

Aunt Jean wished Liffey and Sinead luck and was off in a flash on a shopping spree.

Liffey knew that her aunt normally donated most of her impulsive shopping spree purchases to charity auctions and that buying expensive clothing was her aunt's main form of entertainment. She hoped Aunt Jean would not be wearing anything she bought today and turn up later at the feis wearing some kind of Alaskan fashion statement.

This would be the first time her mother had seen her dance at a feis and Liffey was extremely nervous. She wanted Maeve to be proud of her even though she knew her mother would understand if she had a bad day, and was sure she would always be proud of her. But today, Liffey wanted to deserve it. She was very grateful for all the help her mother had been preparing her and Sinead for this competition and she wanted her mother to "reap the rewards of all her hard work," a phrase her father loved to throw around whenever he could fit it in.

Just as Liffey was pinning the final bobby pin into place to secure her wig, her cell phone text alert went off. This was curious because Aunt Jean had just left, Sinead was standing right next to her and her mother did not know how to text.

She read the message, smiled, and snapped the phone shut.

"Well?" Sinead said.

"Well what?" Liffey answered.

"You know what, Liffey Rivers!"

"Okay. It was John wishing both of us luck."

"Aren't you going to reply?"

"Not now. Later."

Before their discourse could continue, Maeve Rivers returned from the feis with a report:

"It's on schedule downstairs. U-13 is already dancing on both the Novice and Prizewinner stages. Liffey, you're U-14 now so psych yourself up because it looks like your stages are moving right along. Sinead, you're Prelim U-15 stage is a bit slow so you've got some time yet."

"Photo op," Robert Rivers commanded, entering from the adjoining suite's doorway. Sinead and Liffey complied graciously even though they were far too restless to smile much. After taking one photo, he could see that the girls looked nervous and their smiles were forced and offered to "take more photos after you're done dancing."

"Are you going to be with mom downstairs?" Liffey asked, silently praying he had something else to do. "Sorry, to disappoint you, Liffey, but I am meeting Louise and her team in the lobby where most of them are already stationed to work out the final details for Barrow tomorrow."

"Why do we still need all those detectives, Daddy? He's not here at this feis or I would know."

Liffey saw the shadow crossing over her father's face like a dark cloud hiding a bright moon.

"We can't be too careful, Liffey," is all he said before he gave them the victory sign and suddenly walked out of the room.

He was not going to tell Maeve or Liffey that there had been a Special Delivery letter with no return address waiting for them at the front desk when they had checked in.

Louise had put on gloves before he handed over the envelope to her. She immediately took it to the hazardous materials experts at the Anchorage Police Department to rule out the possibility that the anthrax bacteria or some other deadly substance might be enclosed.

The letter was dusted for fingerprints and the police determined there was no sign of *Bacillus anthracis* or other deadly toxin.

There was only a single, scraggly black feather.

***

Even though it was only a small school feis, Liffey was impressed with the quality of the dancing she was watching. Impressed and somewhat intimidated, because she had not expected that there would be so many good dancers here since there were only a few Irish dance schools in all of Alaska. It was obvious that most of the dancers at this feis had been well trained.

Maeve Rivers had worked especially hard with Liffey on her Novice Slip Jig. As Liffey stood in line now waiting for the first ten dancers to be called up on to the stage, she felt the most prepared since she had started competing at feiseanna.

When the stage monitor ushered Liffey and another four dancers on to the plywood platform, Liffey knew she was going to get a first place in this competition. For one thing, she was *totally* ready, because her mother loved the slip jig and had gone over Liffey's for the past six months probably several hundred times. She knew she could do a good slip jig now even if she were sound asleep. Liffey was determined to get into Open Prizewinner in at least two more of her steps at this competition. Her win in St. Louis's Novice Jig competition had put her in Open Prizewinner in the Jig, and her shocking first place in the Novice Hornpipe competition in Pittsburgh, had moved her into the Open dancing level in it as well. All of her other steps were still in Novice.

Sinead had made it to Prelim and Liffey hoped she would be able to watch her dance later. There were twenty dancers, girls and boys, waiting for the U-15 Preliminary Championship competition. It would be difficult to place high in such a large group, but Maeve Rivers had worked hard with Sinead too and Liffey had noticed Sinead's new air of confidence as her strength had returned.

Waiting on the stage while the adjudicator recorded the competitors' numbers, Liffey saw Louise and three of her detectives standing in the crowd. 'When is this all going to end?'

***

After her Slip Jig, the judges recessed for lunch and Liffey raced across the room to the Prelim stage and could not believe her good timing. Sinead was standing on stage ready to dance. Maeve was already there at the stage and Liffey slipped in beside her.

Liffey had been very impressed that Sinead was brave enough to dance again so soon after her brain surgery and radiation treatments. She appeared poised and ready even though Nurse Sheila Sullivan was standing right in front of the stage to observe her patient's every move. Liffey had seen Sheila taking Sinead's and Maeve's vital signs at least three times since they had arrived at the feis hotel.

Sinead saw Liffey and smiled broadly. Liffey flashed her a thumbs up just before the squeezebox musician began to play the Reel music for the soft shoe step in this Preliminary Championship Competition.

Sinead looked good! *Really* good. So good that Liffey thought that her mother's teaching techniques might be supernatural. "Congratulations, Mother! Sinead looks like a world champion!"

***

Liffey realized that things in her life had never been better than they were now. Not even close. Here she was, sitting in a lovely restaurant overlooking Anchorage with her mother, father, best friend and only aunt. They had done a whirlwind tour of the city after the feis and were going to fly to Barrow the next morning, then return for one final night in Anchorage before sailing back to Vancouver again on the *Alaskan Sun.*

205

The Anchorage Feis had been a huge success. Liffey had placed first in her Open Jig, first in her Novice Slip Jig, first in her Novice Reel, second in her Novice Treble Jig and second in her Open Hornpipe.

Liffey had almost cried watching the proud McGowan brothers standing at the results stage trying to keep their composure as they watched their sister receive the beautiful first place trophy and blue sash.

But what had mattered most today, was that Liffey had not only proven to herself that she could be an excellent dancer if she practiced and kept focused, she had also felt love and support like never before.

She had a wonderful family and two good friends now. One of those friends happened to be a boy. Her only regret was seeing how tired and worn out her father was with the stress of trying so hard to keep his family out of harm's way. This had all started because she had let her father down in St. Louis, when she had disobeyed him and pursued a man carrying an Irish dancer doll wearing a sparkling diamond solo dress crown. Since then, things had never been the same.

***

The Anderson detectives were dining at a table in back of the restaurant.

The McGowan brothers had already left for Barrow. Louise was almost certain that there had to be a mole with deep cover inside the Rivers Law Office in Chicago.

How else could their target possibly know which hotel the Rivers were staying at in Anchorage? She hoped the fact that they were going to go to Barrow the next morning had somehow eluded this office mole but she doubted that it had. She knew that their target was more than capable of slipping by her detectives in Barrow.

When she had suggested that Robert Rivers call off their Arctic expedition, he had answered, "I know you can handle this, Louise. I trust you."

She hoped she would prove to be worthy of this trust because she was scared to death.

***

The helicopter pilot hesitated, but Mr. Fields insisted that he be deposited in an open field outside of Barrow where the all-terrain vehicle he had ordered online was waiting for him. He explained that he did not want to fly into the local airport because there had been a bomb threat there a few days ago and it had unnerved him.

There had also been a report of arson in Deadhorse. A recreational vehicle had burned to the ground under very suspicious circumstances. Mr. Fields wanted to keep as far away from the public as he possibly could.

"Well, Mr. Fields, I think this tiny field we are landing in is about as far away from the public as anyone can get. Good luck to you, sir."

Mr. Fields stepped down from the helicopter, ducking as he moved away.

The midnight sun was perfect for middle-of-the-night activity while most people were sleeping. No one would have noticed this helicopter coming and going at 3:00 a.m. When the Rivers family was history, he would drive his all-terrain vehicle over a swampy tundra trail with two stops for necessary supplies at remote outposts. When he reached the closest Inupiat village, he would call his oil company manager and order the helicopter again for a pick up. It would take him to Deadhorse, where a chartered plane would fly him out of Alaska into Canada.

***

This kind of assignment always made Vladimir feel sleazy, like he had sold his soul to the devil. But it was, after all, what he did for a living. The first half of his $150,000 fee had already been paid in cash.

When the car rental agent had closed the office for the night, he stealthily slipped underneath the white minivan in the parking lot reserved for Robert Rivers. It only took him a few minutes to attach the device and a GPS personal locator beacon.

In the morning, he would leave Barrow on the same plane the Rivers would arrive on.

He was to receive the second half of his 'expert' fee in one month—after the sensational story of the tragedy in Barrow had cooled off a bit. It would be delivered to a P.O. Box in Tajikistan in the country's Somoni currency.

***

Robert Rivers had insisted that everyone go to bed at 10:00 p.m. because they had to get up for an early morning flight from Anchorage to Barrow.

"It's supposed to be in the mid-forties in Barrow tomorrow, which will be way above average temperatures for May. It's only twenty-two degrees there today but a veritable heat wave is expected up in Barrow, ladies."

***

Tom Fields sipped his Raven's Brew coffee and was pleased to see that the side compartments of his all-terrain vehicle were stocked with peanut butter, bread, water and gasoline. The GPS seemed to be working. It relayed to him that the van in Barrow was parked in the car rental agency's lot. It was forty degrees, a heat wave here in the middle of the night in the closest city on earth to the North Pole.

37

L iffey could not shake the feeling that something was terribly wrong. She had been looking forward to this part of the trip ever since the *Alaskan Sun* cruise had set off from Vancouver. Now she was irritable and tired from the feis yesterday and the long flight this morning to Barrow had seemed endless. But there was something else as well. A feeling of 'been there, done that' had taken hold of her and she was completely out of sorts.

Sinead, was intently looking out the van window at huge hunks of caribou meat hanging outside of many small block houses whose occupants used the frigid climate to preserve their meat. After awhile, she blurted out: "There are no trees here, Liffey. Can you imagine that? Chunks of meat but no trees!"

Liffey saw her father who was sitting in the front seat next to Jacob, the local Inupiat guide he had hired to take them out to Point Barrow, tense up a bit. She hoped Sinead had not prompted another lecture, but before her father could launch into one, their guide told them, "The nearest tree is three hundred miles south of here."

After a brief drive around Barrow, Jacob suggested that, after they drove out to Point Barrow where they would begin their polar bear expedition, "We can visit the Inupiat Heritage Center. It's probably the best attraction in Barrow, and it will show you much about our ancient Inupiat Eskimo culture—like how we are still permitted to legally hunt whales as we have for thousands of years. They provide us with food, clothing and shelter. After lunch, I will take you to the Center and we'll talk more about it."

Robert Rivers looked in the rearview mirror and saw the dark blue van he had reserved for Louise and her detectives following close behind.

Another car passed them and slowed down directly in front of them. 'Good, the McGowan brothers are on the job now too,' he thought, trying to comfort himself with the fact that they were being escorted front and rear by competent private investigators who were trained to look for anything unusual.

On their drive to Point Barrow, Liffey had a suffocating sensation of *déjà vu*. She could barely pay attention to the interesting facts their guide was dispensing about the melting Arctic Ocean ice and how polar bears were losing their homes on the sea ice where they hunted for seals and gave birth to their cubs.

"With the ice thinning out and much of it melting every year now because of global warming, the unfortunate bears sometimes have to swim for hundreds of miles to find sea ice to hunt from," Jacob said. "Sometimes, their cubs drown trying to keep up with their mother."

Liffey had compiled a list of questions to ask the guide about the impact of global warming on the polar bears living here but was too distracted and restless to retrieve her notebook from her backpack.

The driver slowed down. "I can't remember so many tourists out here in early May before," he said as the vehicles in front and back of him stopped at the shore of the Arctic Ocean looming directly in front of them.

"The word 'traffic' is not in most of our vocabularies here in Barrow," he confided.

"It's almost forty-five degrees now so I think it best to leave your heavy coats in the van while we take a short hike. I cannot remember it ever being this hot over the past nine years since I've been here. The temperature in Barrow is usually below freezing for three hundred and twenty-four days a year."

Sinead asked fearfully, "Are we getting out of the van then, sir?"

"If you like. First, I need to walk ahead to scope out the area. We don't want to get too close to any bears out there. They might just attack us if they are hungry, close by and have the opportunity."

Sinead shuddered. Putting a motherly arm around her shoulders, Maeve said, "You don't have to get out of the van, Sinead. If Aunt Jean had come along with us, I'm sure she would not be getting out. I'm debating about doing it myself."

Liffey was staring at the white arch a few feet in front of the van. Why did it look so *familiar*?

"What is that arch directly in front of us, Jacob?" she asked.

"It's our version of the St. Louis Arch, except ours is the gateway to the North Pole," he laughed.

"It's made of bowhead whale rib cage bones from our whaling expeditions. That's a jawbone there on the ground in the middle of the arch and those are small fishing boats on either side. Many of my people put whale bones on family graves instead of tombstones to mark their burial places."

Liffey and Robert Rivers got out of the van when they saw Jacob's 'all clear' sign to proceed.

Sinead and Maeve opted out.

Liffey stepped over chunks of melting ice on the rocky beach making her way to the arch to touch the whale bones and Robert Rivers walked a few feet ahead with Jacob.

Maybe it was good luck to touch a whale bone? Maybe not. She looked back at the van and waved to Maeve and Sinead.

Out of the corner of her eye, she could see a man who was standing close to the water on an ice mound about half a football field away from the whale arch where she stood. He was gazing up at the sky over the water. There seemed to be something moving behind him.

Liffey looked up and was startled to see a long line of dark, ominous thunderheads rolling towards the shore. A loud assault of thunderclaps began exploding, accompanied by bolts of zigzagging lightning.

The sense of *déjà vu* was almost paralyzing Liffey now and it terrified her. Nothing like this feeling had ever taken hold of her before.

She looked over at the man on the small ice hill who appeared to be mesmerized by the booming thunder and streaks of lightning. The movement behind him took on the shape of a large polar bear.

Liffey was about to shout and try to warn the man about the danger, when she felt a surge of electricity that knocked her down on to her knees.

Had she been struck by lightning? She was having difficulty breathing.

All at once, pins and needles began stinging her entire body like angry bees from a disturbed hive.

She looked at the man again, who was still unaware of the polar bear's presence. He was holding something small in his outstretched hand. It was too far away to see what it was.

A terrible foreboding descended upon Liffey like it was the end of the world and she was watching the sun crashing into the earth, turning everything into a ball of fire.

'This is my *dream*,' she thought sluggishly. 'That's the *Skunk Man* up there, and he is going to detonate a car bomb right now and we are all going to die.'

She struggled to her feet and tried to regain control over her brain which seemed to be turning into slush like the ice melting beneath her.

Everything was in slow motion.

Somehow, she had to get back to the van to warn everyone but she felt like she was being dragged to the bottom of the ocean by a heavy anchor as she tried to move her rubber legs.

The pins and needles were crippling, but she managed to get to the van, pull open the front door and sound the horn.

Maeve shouted: "What's going on?"

Liffey felt a surge of flight adrenaline and jumped out of the van screaming: "Run! Everybody run! There's a bomb under our car!"

She frantically slid open the back door of the van and pulled her dazed mother and a terror-stricken Sinead from it, bellowing: "GET OUT! RUN!"

Louise was there in seconds. "RUN, LOUISE! CAR BOMB!"

Eoin and Michael McGowan arrived next. "RUN!" she shrieked at them, pointing at her mother and Sinead. Both brothers used a fireman's carry to hoist Sinead and Maeve up and across their shoulders before they sprinted away.

When she saw her father and Jacob running towards her from the shoreline, she waved at them frantically to get away and cried out: "CAR BOMB! RUN!"

Liffey felt her legs moving under her again. Holding Louise's hand tightly, she tried to keep pace with her as they bolted away from the van.

Just before she felt the earth shifting underneath her feet and fell to the ground, she turned her head and saw the huge polar bear clawing at the man on the ice mound and then batting him off the hill like an out of the ballpark homerun, into the ocean below.

Lying on the ground after the blast, she thought she saw the bear looking directly at her before everything around her turned dead quiet except for the loud whistling in her ears and the swooshing sound her heart made beating inside her chest.

38

The *Alaskan Sun* sounded its familiar farewell horn blast as it left Seward Harbor.

"I could get used to this cruising life, Liffey," Sinead said from her lounge chair, sipping on a glass of lemonade.

"Me too," Liffey agreed. "It's nice to have your whole world laid out for you on board. You've got your luxurious living space, delicious food, more entertainment than any one person needs in a lifetime, swimming pools, movies and even practice space for Irish dancing."

Sinead sighed. "I wish Luke would text me as often as you hear from John."

"They may be identical twins, Sinead, but I think John got more 'nice' genes."

"Liffey," Sinead asked, "do you mind if I ask you how you manage to cope with everything? I'm still a complete mess from yesterday, but at least I can hear again."

"I'm still a mess too and I never get used to all the trouble that I seem to attract. But it's finally all *over* now, Sinead! Daddy told me they found hard evidence that the Skunk Man is never coming back. He would not tell me exactly what it was, but he said there was absolutely no doubt anymore that mother and I are finally, completely, totally safe."

The *Alaskan Sun* had been sailing along the Inner Passage for a little over an hour when Liffey heard a loud engine noise above her and looked up from her book. She could see that a helicopter was approaching the ship.

"Let's go see who the VIP is, Sinead," Liffey said excitedly.

"Maybe it's somebody we've actually heard of!" Sinead said hopefully.

When Liffey and Sinead reached the helicopter pad, Liffey asked Sinead to stay where she was and walked over to Maeve and Robert Rivers who were already standing near the landing platform. She stood between them, linking their hands together. Sinead called out over the loud engine: "Am I missing something important here? What's going on?"

After the noisy propellers stopped, the passenger door opened and a cheerful looking nun, wearing a light blue habit with a short white veil, stepped down. She beckoned for Robert Rivers to come over and assist her.

"For heaven's sake, Liffey, please tell me *what* is going on here?" Sinead demanded impatiently.

Liffey said, "You'll see," and approached her father, who had already been joined by Maeve, on the landing platform.

Robert Rivers carefully lifted a small boy out of the helicopter on to the platform next to Sister Helen, who handed Neil Rivers his cane with a carved black mamba head. Liffey tried not to shriek with joy as she watched Neil walk, unassisted, a few feet over to a wheelchair that had suddenly appeared and sit down in it.

Maeve knelt alongside, caressing her little boy's head, smiling through the tears which were streaming down her face. Robert Rivers kissed his son on both cheeks and shook hands with him, man-to-man. He lifted Sister Helen up off the deck with a big bear hug.

Liffey rushed over to her brother, tousled his sandy brown hair and said, "Well it's about time you guys turned up! Sister, Sinead and I are going to show my little brother here around the ship a bit before we have our big family reunion back at the suite."

"You're not so big yourself, you know," a small voice chimed in.

Liffey grinned happily and responded, "Fair enough!"

Before anyone present could voice an objection, she commandeered the wheelchair and pushed her beaming little brother away from the helicopter pad towards the Dip'n'Dots counter at the end of the deck.

THE END

A Brockagh Book
www.liffeyrivers.com

MORE LIFFEY RIVERS IRISH DANCER MYSTERIES:

The Mystery of the Sparkling Solo Dress Crown

The Mystery of the Winking Judge

The Secret of the Mountain of the Moon

In the Shadow of the Serpent

Four Mini Mysteries

www.liffeyrivers.com

Made in the USA
San Bernardino, CA
16 December 2014